THAT DOG WON'T HUNT

BRANDILYN COLLINS

DEARING FAMILY SERIES
BOOK 1

Don't miss the interview with Brandilyn at the back of this book, giving a behind-the-scenes look at the Dearing Family and the writing of this story.

~ plus ~

Read the first chapter of Brandilyn's suspense novel *Double Blind*, now available in stores.

PRAISE FOR NOVELS BY BRANDILYN COLLINS

"Excellent novel ... beautifully written ... well developed characters."
--Publishers Weekly, Color the Sidewalk for Me

"Strong writing ... the characters are interesting, and Collins pens some worthy descriptions."
--Publishers Weekly, Capture the Wind for Me

"Collins has written another taut, compelling tale of psychological suspense that weaves a twisty plot with threads of faith."
--Library Journal Starred Review, Double Blind

"Moves along briskly ... the popular novelist's talent continues to flower."
--Publishers Weekly, Gone to Ground

"A taut, heartbreaking thriller ... Collins is a fine writer who knows to both horrify readers and keep them turning pages."
--Publishers Weekly, Over the Edge

"Solidly constructed ... a strong and immediately likeable protagonist ... one of the Top 10 Inspirational Novels of 2010."
--Booklist, Deceit

"A hefty dose of action and suspense with a superb conclusion."
--RT Book Reviews, Exposure

"Intense ... engaging ... whiplash-inducing plot twists."
--Thrill Writer, Dark Pursuit

"A harrowing hostage drama."
--Library Journal, Amber Morn

"One of the Best Books of 2007 ... Top Christian suspense of the year."
--Library Journal Starred Review, Crimson Eve

"A chilling mystery ,,, not one to be read alone at night."
--RT BOOKclub, Coral Moon

"A sympathetic heroine ... effective flashbacks ... Collins knows how to weave faith into a rich tale."
--Library Journal, Violet Dawn

"A master storyteller ... Collins deftly finesses the accelerator on this knuckle-chomping ride."
--RT BOOKclub, Web of Lies

"Finely crafted ... vivid ... another masterpiece that keeps the reader utterly engrossed."
--RT BOOKclub, Dread Champion

"Chilling ... a confusing, twisting trail that keeps pages turning."
--Publishers Weekly, Eyes of Elisha

OTHER BOOKS BY BRANDILYN COLLINS

Southern Contemporary

Bradleyville Series

Cast a Road Before Me
Color the Sidewalk for Me
Capture the Wind for Me

Suspense

Stand Alone Novels

Gone to Ground
Over the Edge
Deceit
Exposure
Dark Pursuit

Rayne Tour YA Series
(co-written with Amberly Collins)

Always Watching
Last Breath
Final Touch

Kanner Lake Series

Violet Dawn
Coral Moon
Crimson Eve
Amber Morn

Hidden Faces Series

Brink of Death
Stain of Guilt
Dead of Night
Web of Lies

Chelsea Adams Series

Eyes of Elisha
Dread Champion

Non-Fiction

Getting Into Character:
Seven Secrets a Novelist Can Learn From Actors

CHAPTER 1

Have mercy, a smell like this in the house could cost Ben his new fiancée. And he and Christina were likely to pull up any minute.

It had been hard enough for Ruth Dearing to keep the place straightened with three daughters—two of them with husbands and kids—already home for the family summer reunion. Noise and purses and sunglasses and toys everywhere. Ruth lived for her family to come home. But today things had to look just so. Wasn't every time that Ben, their youngest, brought home a young woman he said he was going to marry. A "quiet" gal, he'd told Ruth and Sy. "Kinda reserved." In other words, everything the Dearing family was not. To put it mildly.

Ho boy.

Christina could easily be overwhelmed at this gathering, but no one else in the family seemed the least bit worried. Least of all Ben. But Ruth had been young once, and yes—shy. Even though she and Syton had been in love since high school, Ruth remembered all too well that nerve-wracking first meeting with his parents. Sy's family had a lot more money than her own, and his parents seemed so intimidating. Still, she'd only had to meet the two of them. Imagine being shoved into *this* family. Ruth had already warned her daughters to be mindful of Christina's shyness. And she'd flown about the house today, trying to make everything look perfect.

Now this horrible stench.

Nose wrinkled, Ruth strode to the doorway leading to the house's west wing, which contained the grandkids' play room. "Pogey, get in here and put these shoes on! They're stinkin' the kitchen to high heaven!"

At Ruth's feet, Lady Penelope, her and Sy's finicky Yorkie, whined. Poor Penny lay on the floor with her paws practically over her nose. Ruth picked her up.

"How *do* y'all stand that smell?" Ruth turned and frowned at her three daughters playing an animated game of cards in the adjoining family room.

Sarah, Pogey's mother, sighed. "I'm used to it. Kid's got the smelliest feet this side of the Mississippi."

"More like in the whole country." Maddy placed a card on the table.

"Ah! Liverpool Rummy!" Sarah snatched up the card and laid down her hand, face alight.

"Girl, you are a cheat and a half." Jess's clear voice sliced across the room.

2

"I am not. You're just lousy at this game."

"I'm not lousy at anything, thank you very much."

"Oh, yeah?" Sarah smirked at Maddy. "Remember when she tried to take up the hem of her own prom dress?"

Maddy let out her staccato laugh. "Yeah, she quit about the time it was up to her thighs."

"Oh, can it, y'all." Jess threw down her cards. "Besides, Sarah, you were long gone from home then, so how would you know?"

"I had Maddy to feed me information, that's how."

Ruth shook her head. Sarah was now thirty-nine, Maddy, thirty-four, and Jess, thirty-two. Loved each other like crazy. But they could still argue just like in the old days.

Ruth turned back toward the play room. She could hear her grandson's video game still going. At age ten that kid had the fastest thumbs of anyone alive. The girls—Lacey, six, and Alex, five—were quiet as church mice. Probably still coloring. Most of the time those two young cousins got along famously—until they didn't.

"Pogey!"

"Comin'."

Sarah pushed back her chair and sashayed into the kitchen. "I beat know-it-all Jess again," she sing-songed. "For the *fourth* time."

Jess huffed.

Sarah picked up her son's offending footwear and made a face. "Pogey, get in here!"

"Okay."

"Try makin' it in this lifetime!"

The video game silenced. Pogey appeared in the hall, heaving a sigh. He was short for his age, round-

3

cheeked and freckle-faced. Somewhat pudgy. Pogey wore every emotion on his sleeve. As he approached, barefoot, Ruth braced herself for further smells. Penny buried her little doggie snout in Ruth's chest.

Sarah held the shoes out to her son. "How long since you washed those feet?"

"I took a shower last night." Pogey's voice rose in his best "Why me?" tone.

"You know you have to wash 'em twice a day in the summer. Go stick 'em in the tub." Sarah shoved the shoes into his hands. "And take these outside to the hose."

"Then they'll be all wet."

"Not for long. Just leave 'em in the sun."

The July day in Justus, Mississippi was steaming hot.

Muttering to himself, Pogey took his shoes and trudged through the kitchen toward the bedroom wing of Ruth and Sy's rambling house.

Stinky feet and hating to bathe were not a good mix.

Ruth looked to Maddy. "Can you girls put up that card table now? Ben and Christina are fixin' to be here soon." And where were Sy and his two sons-in-law, Jake and Don? They should've been home and cleaned up from their golf game by now. The whole family needed to be here to welcome the new fiancée.

Sarah patted her mother on the shoulder. "Relax. You don't need to be so worried about this."

Maddy stood and began gathering the cards on the table. "Yeah, Mama. This family's hardly perfect. The sooner Christina figures that out, the sooner she'll start to fit in. Right, Jess?"

"Speak for yourself about the perfect part."

4

Ruth pursed her mouth. Why did her family always accuse her of worrying? It was just that Ben had sounded so ecstatic on the phone when he told her about Christina. "I know we haven't been datin' long, Mama," he said, "but this woman is so incredible. I love her like crazy, and I want to be with her forever. I want her to meet the family and fit right in."

Just a little pressure.

"I am *not* worried."

"Uh-huh." Sarah gestured with her chin toward the Yorkie. "Then why're you holding Penny so tight?"

The dog *was* squirming. Ruth put her down. Penny headed for her bed in the piano corner, nose in the air. She turned in circles on the plush yellow fabric, then flopped down, facing the wall. She'd had enough of humans for a while.

Ruth's gaze cruised the clean kitchen, searching for anything amiss. She spotted a glass on the counter and walked over to put it in the dishwasher.

Maddy and Jess turned the card table on its side.

"I still say Ben's too young to get married." Jess folded in the first metal leg with a *clack*. "Besides that he tends to fall too hard, too fast. He hardly knows this girl. And *she's* only twenty-three."

Sarah leaned against the kitchen counter. "Oh, don't get started on the too-young thing again."

"Well, it's true."

"Ben's twenty-seven. And he makes very good money."

"He has no idea how to take care of a wife. *He's* the one who still needs takin' care of."

As the baby of the family and the only boy, Ben had certainly been catered to by his three older

5

sisters. Especially Jess, who was five when he was born. From his birth she'd considered herself Ben's second mother.

Maddy folded in another table leg. "All wives take care of their husbands. Don would never make it without me."

"But he takes care of *you* too." Ruth picked up a sponge to wipe the spotless counter. "That's how a good marriage works—each puttin' the other first."

Jess threw Maddy a look. "That's why I'm not married. I have no intention of takin' care of some man."

"Lord help the man who marries *you*." Sarah wagged her head. "You're as argumentative as a lawyer."

"I *am* a lawyer."

"Not to mention as picky as Lady Penelope."

Penny's ears pricked, but she refused to turn around.

"Yeah?" Jess punched in the last table leg. "And the whole family kowtows to that dog just to keep her happy. Sounds good to me."

Ruth stopped her sponging. "Don't call Penny a dog—she might hear you."

Maddy humphed. "Don't expect *me* to do any kowtowing in your direction."

"Me either," Sarah said.

The front door opened. Ruth froze. "Is that Ben?"

Jess walked over to stick her head out the family room doorway. "It's Pogey, carryin' his shoes outside." The door slammed shut. Jess waved a hand in front of her nose. "Whew. You can tell he's been through here."

"You casting aspersions on my son?" Sarah said.

"With those feet, he manages that all on his own."

6

"Careful, little sister. You'll have kids, too, someday."

Jess rolled her eyes. "In the next millennium, maybe."

Maddy picked up the card table. "Listen, Jess, don't you dare be hard on Christina."

"So now we're talking about Christina? And why should I be hard on her anyway?"

"Oh, I don't know. Maybe 'cause the last time Ben brought a girl home you sent her packin' in less than twenty-four hours."

"I did not. They had a fight."

"*You* caused it."

Ruth went back to wiping the counter—harder. She was staying out of this one.

Jess snorted. "And just what did I do?"

Sarah put a finger to her cheek. "What do you think, Maddy? Was it tellin' the girl her roots needed done within two minutes of meetin' her? Or maybe fillin' her ears with not-so-flattering stories of 'Baby Ben.'"

Maddy slid the card table behind the couch. "No, no, it was sneakin' bacon into her omelet."

Jess raised her arms. "Who doesn't eat bacon?"

"She was vegetarian, Jess, and you knew it."

"Well, there ya go." Jess looked to her mother for support. Ruth kept wiping. "No vegetarian would ever last in this family. What would we do at reunions, grill tofu instead of ribs? That girl wasn't right for Ben, and y'all know it. *I* was the only one willin' to do somethin' about it."

"Maybe you should've let Ben decide that." Sarah wagged her head.

The counter sparkled. Ruth moved to the stove.

7

"He *did*." Jess's voice lightened. "Soon as he had his eyes opened."

Ruth set down the sponge and faced her youngest daughter. She couldn't keep quiet any longer. "Jess, your sisters are right. You need to go easy on Christina. Like you said, she's young. And she's an only child, so she's hardly used to all the goin's in this house."

"Oh, I'll be sweet as pie, Mama. You act like I'm some hardhearted thing."

"No, you're far from that. But sometimes you talk first and think later."

"Yeah, Jess." Maddy plopped down on the couch. "Like puttin' the cart before the egg."

Jess squinted. "Huh?" She, Sarah, and Ruth stared at Maddy, trying to figure what she'd said. Then they burst into cackles.

Maddy wrinkled her brow. "What'd I say now?"

"You said ..." Sarah held her sides. She stumbled over to the kitchen table and collapsed into a chair.

"*What?*"

"C-cart before the ..." Giggles bubbled out of Sarah. "Egg."

"Oh, Maddy." Jess folded over, hands on her knees. "That's your best one yet."

"Mom!" Maddy turned to Ruth, like she used to do as a kid. "They're makin' fun of me again."

Ruth fell into a chair beside Sarah, laughing too hard to answer. For years Maddy had spouted mixed metaphors, never realizing what she'd said. She could come up with some doozies. But Jess was right—this one took the cake.

Oh, goodness, Ruth's sides hurt.

8

Sarah wiped her eyes. "Maddy, darling, it's cart before the horse. Or which came first, the chicken or the egg?"

Maddy pulled in her mouth. "Well, mine's much better."

Ruth and Maddy's two sisters started laughing all over again.

"Fine then, y'all just cackle away." Maddy strode through the kitchen toward the play room. "I'm gonna go sit with the girls."

Poor Maddy. Ruth worked her mouth, trying to get hold of herself. She almost made it—until she caught Sarah's eye. They fell into chortles all over again.

Maddy called from down the hall. "I still hear you!"

A faint rumbling sounded in Ruth's ears—the garage door rolling up. "Oh." She hiccupped and straightened. It still took time to get herself under control. "The boys are home." Finally.

A sudden wail exploded from the play room. "That's *my* page!" Alex's high voice.

"It's not, I saw it first!" Lacey.

"Stop it, you two." Maddy sounded extra firm, likely still irritated over being laughed at. "There's plenty coloring books."

"I had it *first*!" Alex insisted.

At the end of the long hall, the door leading into the garage opened. Male voices sounded in a friendly argument about the golf game.

Lacey shrieked. The men's voices cut off.

Ruth hurried toward the play room, meeting her husband, Sy, in the hall. He was solidly built and stood at six-two, a good foot taller than she. Fortunately the girls had gotten his height. Sy was

9

flushed and sweaty, his thick gray-white hair damp at the ends. But that face of his—the face she'd loved since high school—was just as handsome. Sy's blue eyes met hers. "What's goin' on?"

Ruth lifted a shoulder.

He stuck his head into the play room. "Hey!" The word boomed. "Who's yellin' in here?"

Ruth came up behind him and peered into the room. "It's Lacey." Alex folded her arms. "She stole my colorin' page."

Sy drew to his full height in the doorway, one hand on either side of the threshold. "I got an idea. I can take all your colorin' books and send you to your rooms. That what you want?"

That was Ruth's Sy. Loving and compassionate— and a strong disciplinarian.

Alex gave one of her famous pouts, her light eyebrows practically meeting. She swooshed a golden strand of hair off her face. "No."

"No either." Lacey glared at the table.

"All right then. Stop fightin', or I'm back here faster 'n' a hot knife through butter."

The girls eyed each other, then silently picked up crayons. Maddy mouthed *Thank you* to her dad. She definitely had her problems with making her daughter, Alex, behave at times.

The three men and Ruth headed into the kitchen, Maddy following. She poked her husband in the shoulder. "How'd you do?" At five-ten, Don stood only about an inch taller than his wife. His sandy hair had a buzz cut, and his blaze-blue eyes looked even bluer against a summer tan.

"Great. Won the game, of course."

10

Jake, Sarah's husband, shook his head. "Only because you moved the ball that time." Jake was an insurance salesman—and looked the part. Tall and lanky, he had jet black hair and wore wire rim glasses.

"I did not move a ball."

"I *saw* you. Didn't he, Sy?"

Sy raised his hands. "Don always moves a ball. That's how he wins."

Don shot them both looks. "You guys just can't stand to lose."

Jake and Sy answered at the same time, and soon all three men were trying to out-talk each other. Out spilled the story of their long, hot golf game, and who shot what on which hole—no, that was an exaggeration—no, it was not. Soon Sarah and Maddy joined in, and the noise level rose. Ruth could only laugh—then cover her ears. She loved having all the family home, but oh, the hullaballoo! The kitchen filled with the smell of sweaty men on top of the lingering odor of Pogey's sneakers. In the midst of all that, another shriek came from the play room, followed by a hissed "Be quiet, you want Granddad to take our colors?"

The phone rang. Somehow Ruth managed to hear it. She wound through all the bodies in the kitchen to answer. "Hello?" She put a hand over her other ear to shut out the mayhem.

"Hey, Mama!" It was Ben. "Just lettin' you know we're a few miles from the house."

"Oh." *Oh, no.* The family wasn't ready. The men still sweaty, Lacey and Alex mad at each other, Pogey's smelliness still lingering, and everyone carrying on ...

11

"Mama? You got a party goin' on there without me?" Ben's mock indignation wrapped around an obvious grin. He sounded so excited, happier than Ruth had heard him for a long time. Ruth could picture him in his car, telling Christina how great everything would be. Ben had a way of looking at the world through rose-colored glasses—and could be surprised and hurt when things turned gray.

Oh, Lord, please let this all work out.

"Well, you know how it is." She nearly had to shout.

"So get 'em all out on the lawn to meet my Christina. The grand moment's here, and I want to see y'all lined up nice and pretty."

Nice and pretty? Ho boy.

CHAPTER 2

Panic rolled in Christina Day's stomach.

"And this is our downtown, all two blocks of it." Ben Dearing slouched in the driver's seat of his sporty white BMW, one hand on the wheel—his typical casual driving pose. But his tanned face was all smiles. Ben had been like an over-the-top kid ever since they left Dallas that morning. Couldn't wait to show Christina off to his family, he said. Couldn't wait to show his family off to her.

Now he'd just called and asked them all to be out on the lawn as the two of them drove up.

Was he crazy?

How was she supposed to handle meeting them all at once? Everybody looking her up and down, judging her. Like a ratty dress in some fancy shop window. And this was only Friday. They had all day

Saturday and Sunday here, not leaving until Monday morning.

Why hadn't she found some excuse not to come?

It could be worse. If this was an extended family reunion, with grandparents and aunts and uncles and cousins, she *wouldn't* have come. But Ben had told her his grandparents had all passed away. A very sad thing for all of them. And the cousins and uncles and aunts didn't live close.

Still, the immediate Dearing family was more than enough.

With a trembling hand, Christina pulled down the visor to check her reflection in the mirror. She looked awful, as usual. Bad hair day, makeup sloppy. Eyes all scared-looking. Oh, yeah, this was going to be some great meeting.

"Stop worryin' about what you look like—you're gorgeous." Ben patted her leg.

Christina put the visor back up.

She *wasn't* gorgeous. Had never been, no matter what Ben said. Her father had called her Ugly Bug for as long as she could remember, always with a sneer. Sometimes she'd wished she *was* a bug, so she could crawl away from her parents for good.

Nothing like Ben's family.

During the whole six-hour trip from Dallas he'd told Christina all about his "wonderful, wacky" older sisters and their little town of Justus, Mississippi. These were on top of the stories she'd already heard in their two and a half months of dating. Christina loved the stories, soaking them up like a bone-dry sponge. A family that really loved each other. Talked to each other. Wanted to *be* with each other. The Dearings sounded like they lived on a different planet.

14

Wherever it was, Christina wanted to be on it. Even as she knew deep down that would likely never work. And what would happen when she didn't fit in? She'd told Ben nothing of her abusive past. Just that she was an only child. That she didn't talk to her parents much since moving out. At first she hadn't dared tell Ben anything for fear of scaring him away. Why should he want damaged goods, especially with the childhood he had? Then the closer they grew, the more she had to lose, and she *really* couldn't tell. When Ben tried to get more out of her she'd just turn the conversation back to his family.

"So, come on—what do you think of our busy downtown?" Ben threw her another grin, his blue eyes sparkling. Those eyes could light up a room. And Ben's friendly, boyish face drew everyone to him. That and lots of charm.

Christina tried to concentrate on the near-empty streets. She took in a drugstore and grocery, a dry cleaners, a barbershop. Some other small businesses. Didn't look like much. She'd never lived in a small town. Four thousand people, where everybody knew everybody else's business? Sounded scary. But Justus was Ben's hometown, and for that reason Christina wanted to love it.

"I'm trying to picture you here as a boy."

Nice deflective answer. She was good at that.

He laughed. "I had a lot of chocolate shakes at the drugstore counter. They still make 'em. I'll bring you back down for one."

"Promise?"

"You bet." Ben reached for her hand and squeezed it.

15

Christina's heart surged. Everything about this guy was incredible—his solid childhood and sense of family, the feel of his arms around her, the way he looked at her when she spoke. Not to mention his smarts in computer programming. Yet he was so laid back. That easy confidence was what first had attracted Christina to him. But—get in line, everyone at work loved Ben. She was just a lowly new admin at the huge company where they worked. She'd never in the world expected him to notice her. When he asked her out, she about fell off her chair. Wasn't worth a thing the rest of the day.

Now he'd asked her to marry him. *Marry* him. Her hopeless life had just blitzed into a Cinderella fairy tale. She had to make it last, somehow, some way.

Ben pointed with his chin. "See that Corner Café sign? We turn there and head out of town. The house is in half a mile."

Christina's panic squirmed harder.

She'd seen pictures of the house. It was so pretty—a large white two-story with a big porch framed by round pillars, long wings on either side. What an amazing place to grow up. Nothing like the crummy duplex she'd lived in.

"Come on, Christina, smile. You look like a deer in headlights."

She curved her mouth.

"There ya go."

She breathed in ... out. Ben said his family teased a lot. That's how they "loved on" each other. Christina didn't understand teasing. When her parents had said something, they meant it. And it was never nice. To her, teasing felt like put-downs, and

16

she couldn't stand conflict. She'd had enough of that in her life.

A dark memory filled her head, one of many that could rise at any time. Her father yelling. *"When I tell you to get me a beer, I mean now!" Christina was nine and could barely walk. He'd whipped her back and legs so hard that morning, they'd bled. The buckle had gouged out pieces of skin. Now her body screamed with every step. Somehow she managed to get to the refrigerator and back. Her father snatched the bottle from her hand. "Ain't you happy to be servin' your daddy, Ugly Bug?"*

Christina lowered her chin and mumbled, "Yes."

"What?"

"Yes!"

"That's better." He sneered. "And put a smile on your face when you're talkin' to me. Or I'll take that belt to you again."

Christina spread her lips wide — a clown smile she didn't begin to feel ...

She blinked out of the memory and shivered. "What if your family doesn't like me?"

"Are you kidding? They'll love you."

"What if they don't?"

They reached the Corner Café. Ben turned right. He threw her a puzzled glance. "Why do you always see the negative side of things?"

Maybe because her entire life had gone wrong until she met Ben? You didn't grow up the way she did and just suddenly decide to trust that life would be good.

"I'm not negative. Just ... cautious."

"Well, you don't need to be cautious here. Just be yourself."

Which "self" would that be? The one who knew she'd never measure up to Ben and was scared to

17

death of the day he realized it? The girl who wondered if she really knew how to love? It definitely wouldn't be the bitter kid who'd grown up determined never to be trampled on again. That one was way too harsh. That person rattled around inside Christina, but she always pushed her down. Was too scared to let her out.

Christina's nerves prickled. She turned away to focus outside the window. Houses soon gave way to a rural road and green fields. It was all so pretty. Made her chest ache.

"You know you'll do great." Ben's voice softened. "Really, Chris."

Christina. My name's Christina.

"I so want you to be happy. I want you to love them."

Christina faced Ben and forced another smile. "I'm sure I will."

But would they love *her?* Even Ben wouldn't, if he really knew her. He was all filled up inside. She was empty. He was positive and strong. She was anxious and weak. Everything Ben and his family were, she wasn't. It was one thing to hide the real Christina from Ben. But how to hide from an entire family? Ben was so close to them. What would he do if someone didn't like her? Wouldn't he think twice? He had twenty-seven years' history with his parents and sisters, ten weeks with her.

They rounded a corner—and the Dearings' beautiful house came into view. On the lawn stood a whole group of people. Christina immediately recognized the three sisters. Sarah, with the Dearing's signature chestnut brown hair cut short. Maddy, wearing hers long and straight. And Jess, who bleached her hair blond and cut it shoulder length.

"There they are!" Ben gave a huge wave, and they all waved back. Two darling little girls in front jumped up and down. Christina knew the bigger one was Lacey, Sarah's daughter. She'd seen pictures of the little girl with her incredible hair, all in brown ringlets to her shoulders.

Here they all were — Ben's family. Supposed to be *her* new family.

Christina pasted on a smile and managed to raise a feeble hand.

CHAPTER 3

Jess stood close to the driveway, ready as the first to greet her little brother with a big smile. Penance, in a way. After the last girlfriend he'd brought home, Ben hadn't spoken to Jess for four months. Which was ages in the Dearing family. He'd blamed her for his argument with the girl that ended in their breakup. Only later did he admit Jess had been right. Still, that hadn't stopped him from calling her cell last night. "Listen, Jess, you got to take it easy on Chris, okay? She really is shy, and I don't want you grillin' her with questions or makin' your I-can-see-right-through-you comments."

Jess bit her tongue. So she could read people well. Was that a bad thing?

"You hear me?"

"I hear you. Good grief, I'm not an ogre."

"No, you just ... spout what you think. And sometimes it makes you sound like an ogre."

"Gee, thanks."

"I didn't mean—"

"Thing is, Ben, you're my adored little brother, you know that. Sarah, Maddy, and I—we've all looked after you. They've managed to find good husbands, and we want you to find a good wife. Be happy. Stay married the rest of your life."

"You don't think I can do that?"

"Of course you can." Jess's mouth curved. "You just might need my help a little."

"*Jessica*—"

"Okay, okay. Just teasing."

Well. She'd been half teasing.

Now as Ben's car pulled into the driveway, Jess caught her first glimpse of Christina. Whoa. Jess raised her eyebrows as she plastered on a smile. The girl was gorgeous. Long straight blonde hair—*real* blonde—and an oval face. No wonder Ben had been attracted the moment he first saw her.

"Hi, Ben!" Mama slipped to Jess's side, her face alight. She patted her palms together in anticipation.

"Hang in there, Mama, everything will be just fine."

"Of course it will be." Mama's words were over-emphatic, as if she hadn't a clue why Jess had made the comment.

"Hi, Ben, hi, Christina!" Sarah and Maddy called. The rest of the family crowded forward. Jake was taking pictures.

"Look, she's pretty." Lacey pointed at Christina. Alex nodded, her mouth a round O.

Ben stopped the car and popped open his door. Christina started to open hers, but Ben laid a hand on her arm. She stilled.

He strode around the front of the car and wrapped Mama in a bear hug. The top of her head didn't even reach his chin. Ben gave Jess a quick hug next, then stepped back. "And now"—he opened the passenger door with a flourish—"meet the most wonderful girl in the world, Christina Day!"

Oh, sheesh. Was that terror that flashed across the girl's face?

Christina smiled, and whatever Jess had seen—if anything at all—was gone. "Hi, everyone!" Christina got out of the car and stood next to Ben, his arm slipping around her waist. She looked a tad pale, and something about her smile slipped.

Okay. It *was* terror.

"Christina, so nice to meet you!" Mama held out her arms. "We're very glad to have you with us."

"Glad to be here."

Really? Didn't look like that to Jess.

Christina hesitated, then let Mama give her a hug. She stiffened in Mama's arms. Surely Mama felt it, but she gave no sign.

"And this is my sister, Jess." Ben pushed Christina forward. "The one you don't wanna get into an argument with." He grinned.

"Oh, knock it off, Ben." Jess turned to Christina. "Hi. So glad to meet you." She didn't offer a hug. Poor girl apparently had enough to handle. Jess looked into her turquoise eyes. What a color. And her makeup was perfect. Long, mascaraed eyelashes, but not overdone. Pink lipstick. Looked like she should be on a magazine cover.

So why did she seem so unsure of herself?

23

Christina dipped her head. "Glad to meet you, too."

"Can I see your ring?" Jess pointed to Christina's left hand. Christina smiled shyly and held out her fingers. She sported a large sparkly diamond, simple but elegant. "Oh, it's lovely."

"Thanks."

"I want to see too." Mama came close to look. Soon Christina was holding her hand out for all to admire.

"It's beautiful." Mama patted Christina on the shoulder. "Good choice, Ben."

"Thanks, Mama." Ben was absolutely beaming. He pointed his fiancée toward the rest of the family.

"This is Maddy, the middle sister. And Sarah, the oldest ..." Ben made his way through the family, pulling an ever-smiling Christina along with him. Jess thought the girl's lips just might break. "And this"—Ben's voice took on obvious pride—"is my father."

Dad hugged his son and laid a hand on Christina's shoulder. "Welcome to the family."

She looked up at him, swallowing hard. Then covered it with a downright beatific smile. "Thank you."

Ben went through brothers-in-law Jake and Don, over to Pogey, and ended with Lacey and Alex.

Lacey looked up at Christina with round chocolate eyes. "You're pretty."

Christina blinked. "Thank you." Her voice softened. She stooped down and took the little girl's hands in hers. "And so are you."

Lacey beamed. "Are you and Uncle Ben gettin' married?"

"Yes."

24

"Can I be in the wedding?"

"Now, Lacey." Ben to the rescue. "We can talk about that later."

"But can I?"

"Later, Lace."

Lacey pulled in the sides of her mouth. Christina winked at her.

Christina turned next to Alex and reached for her hands. "Here's another pretty one."

Alex jerked away. Christina let go immediately, her expression flattening. Her palms sprang up as if to say *So sorry!*

She stood up, looking stricken.

"Alex is just a little shy." Ben ruffled his niece's hair. She pulled away and frowned at him.

Christina nodded. But Jess had the distinct impression she was berating herself, as if she'd committed the unpardonable sin.

Mama stepped to Christina's side. "Well, let's get you out of this heat and show you to your room."

"Oh, I should get my things out of the car."

"Don't worry, the men will get them."

Christina tipped back her head to admire the house. "It's so beautiful."

"Glad you like it. The place is kind of old now, but we love it. Raised all four kids here."

Good ol' Mama, with her natural warmth and love for people. If anyone could make this new addition to the family feel at home, it was Mama.

But as far as Jess was concerned, things weren't looking so good. As much as Christina might have the rest of the family fooled, to Jess she looked like she'd just as soon be cleaning toilets. Or be holed up in a cave. Jess glanced at Ben and caught him looking at Christina, love shining in his eyes.

Oh, man. He'd fallen hard.

Mama and Christina crossed the porch and went inside the house, most of the family following. Ben turned to the car to get bags, Don saying he'd help. Jess trailed along. "What can I carry?"

"There's not much. We packed light." Ben handed her Christina's purse—a white tote, neatly packed. Don took one suitcase from the trunk. Ben took the second.

Ben fell alongside Jess as they headed for the porch. "So what do you think? Isn't she gorgeous?"

"She really is, Ben."

"She's just the best. I'm so lucky. I can't wait to get married."

"When's the wedding?"

"Haven't figured that out yet. We all have to talk about it so everyone can be there."

"What about *her* family?"

"She doesn't have any. Not to speak of anyway."

What? "How can she not have family?"

"Well, I mean she doesn't talk to her parents. I don't know why."

Jess eyed her brother, shocked. "Don't you think it's a little bit important to find out why? Family's a big deal. It's *who* a person is."

"I know her, Jess." Ben's voice edged with defensiveness. "I know she's a wonderful person."

Yeah, he'd known her for a whole ten weeks. Still, ten weeks was plenty enough time to at least talk about family.

Something wasn't right here.

They reached the porch steps. Jess stopped and Ben lingered with her. "Tell me—why do you love her?"

26

He looked at his sister as if she'd just sprouted a second nose. "Why wouldn't I? She's incredible."

"I know, but I mean ... what exactly is incredible about her? Other than her looks."

Anger flicked across Ben's face. "*Why* do you always do this? You're so—"

"Please, Ben. I'm just tryin' to understand how this happened so fast."

Ben's jaw slowly relaxed. He sighed. "Okay. She's a great listener, for one. And she's really smart. Main thing is—she loves me so much. It's a wonderful feelin' to have someone so excited to be with me. To want to marry me."

Wait—he loved her because she loved him?

Terrific.

Ben laid a hand on Jess's arm. "Listen, I don't want to fight about this. And I don't want you all over her. I'm tellin' you—she's the one. Really. It's right this time."

Uh-huh.

Jess looked up at the little brother she loved so fiercely. When he'd been bullied in the first grade, she was there to protect him. When he had his first heartbreak over some girl at age eleven, she'd been the one to console. Not to mention all his other heartbreaks during high school. He was just too trusting. And he had such a big heart. But how to protect Ben from himself now that he was an adult?

"I just don't want you hurt." Unexpected tears bit at Jess's eyes.

"No way." He threw her a wide smile. "Not this time. This one's perfect."

27

CHAPTER 4

"Here's your room, Christina, down at the end of the hall." Mrs. Dearing extended her hand toward the last doorway on the right.

Christina peeked inside and saw lush red carpet and drapes with gold-colored bedding. The furniture was white, trimmed in gold. There was even a lovely padded bench with brass scrolled legs and arms. A doorway on the opposite side led to a private bathroom.

"Oh. It's so … it's *beautiful.*"

Ruth smiled. "It's our one real guestroom. The others are all the kids' old rooms."

"Do the little girls or Pogey need to stay in here? I could sleep on a couch or something."

Ruth waved a hand. "Don't even think of it. The girls sleep on the floor in their parents' rooms, and Pogey's on the sofa in the play room. This is for *you.*"

29

Christina's throat tightened. This was so pretty, she could stay in here all day.

Ben brought her suitcase and purse down the hall. "Like it?" He gestured toward the doorway.

"It's wonderful."

He walked inside and dropped her bags on the bed. "Good." He smiled at her, and Christina smiled back. His mom smiled at both of them.

An awkward second hung in the air.

"Well." Mrs. Dearing backed up a step. "I'll let you get settled in, Christina. I need to head into the kitchen."

"What's for supper tonight, Mama?" Something akin to teasing laced Ben's words.

"Ribs, of course. What else would we have the first night everyone's home?"

Christina looked to her fiancé, eyebrows raised.

He shrugged. "Summer reunion tradition."

Of course. This family must be full of traditions. Christina felt another twinge of panic. She'd have to learn them all. Participate in them all. Not to mention remember everyone's name in the family and try to be their friend.

A sense of overwhelming rose in her lungs. She pushed it back down.

"I'm gonna take my stuff upstairs to my room. I'll see you in a bit." Ben leaned over and kissed her. "I love you."

"I love *you.*"

Behind her closed door, Christina plopped down on the bed. She held out her hand and examined her engagement ring. So beautiful. She still couldn't believe she wore it.

If only she could just stay in this pretty room and hide awhile. Meeting the whole family at once had

30

felt like running through a gauntlet. And Sarah's husband—what was his name?—had been taking pictures! Christina would look terrible in them. What would supper be like, with everyone at the table? What if they asked about her parents? What could she possibly say?

Christina pushed to her feet and examined her face in the mirror. Her makeup needed fixing. And maybe she should change her top—

Somebody knocked on her door.

She closed her eyes for a split second, then moved to open it. Lacey stood before her, carrying a darling little Yorkie in her arms. The dog regarded Christina with intelligent brown eyes—*Who are you?* Her silky fur was blonde-white, her ears a golden brown. A pink elastic band held a little knot of hair sticking straight up on the top of her head. Around her neck was a pink bling collar dangling a matching pink crown. Her tiny front paws draped over Lacey's arm.

"This is Lady Penelope." Lacey spoke as if presenting royalty. "But we call her Penny."

Ben had told Christina about his parents' beloved dog. They'd gotten her seven years ago, two years after he'd moved out to attend college—the last kid gone. "My Mama was so lonely she wanted a dog to replace me." Ben had laughed. "My dad says fine, get a big dog. Mama sets her sights on this tiny puppy who'd fit in her pocket. Dad takes one look at Penny and says, 'Ruthie, that dog won't hunt.' Southern way of sayin' it makes no sense, ain't gonna work. Now my dad's totally in love with that pooch."

"Oh, Lacey, she's so cute!" Christina's heart turned over. She'd have given anything to have a dog like this when she was young. "Do you think she'd let me hold her?"

"I don't know, she's kind of ... partic ... somethin'."

"Particular?"

"Uh-huh."

"I see." Christina shifted on her feet, not sure what to say next. "You want to bring her inside?"

Lacey thought it over. "Maybe if I put her on your bed and you sat down, she could figure you out."

"Okay." Christina backed up and sat. Lacey lowered Penny onto the gold bedcover. The dog cocked her head at Christina, then inched forward to sniff. Christina held out her fingers.

"She likes you." Lacey sounded relieved.

"You think?" Christina didn't dare move her hand.

"Uh-huh. Or else she'd just walk away."

They watched the Yorkie. After a moment she lay down with a little *chuff*.

"I think you can try to pet her now."

Christina glanced at Lacey, then raised her hand toward Penny's head. She did a few cautious scratches. Penny's eyes half-closed.

"See, she *does* like you."

Christina scratched more. The Yorkie's hair was so soft.

"I'm in dancing lessons." Lacey hunched one shoulder forward. "Want to see?"

"Sure."

Lacey slid off the bed and moved to the center of the room, where she pushed up on the toes of her sneakers.

"Wow, that's terrific. I can't stand like that."

"Mm-hm." Lacey moved forward a few steps. "I can walk, too."

32

"That's amazing."

She minced a few more steps, then came down off her toes. "It's not all the way on my toes, though, like the bigger girls. It's more like half way. I can't get the real toe shoes until I'm ten or eleven."

"Oh. Why's that?"

"'Cause teacher says my toes aren't flat yet. When I'm ten or eleven they'll be right."

"I see."

Lacey sat back down on the bed. "Do you dance?"

"No, afraid not."

"Your parents didn't give you lessons?"

What a thought. "No."

Lacey cocked her head. "Do you wish they did?"

Christina wished a lot of things. "Yes, because then I could dance with you."

"I can teach you."

"That would be great."

Lacey opened her mouth and gave a huge, satisfied sigh. "You're my friend, aren't you." It wasn't a question.

Christina's heart surged. She placed her hand underneath the little girl's delicate chin. "You bet I am."

Lacey grinned.

Ben appeared in the doorway. "Hey, what're you two doin'?"

His niece lifted her head and gave Ben an imperious look. "Girl stuff."

Ben's mouth twitched. "Oh. Well, come on out, Chris, and be with the rest of the family."

Christina's gaze slid to Lacey. The little girl stared back, as if looking right into Christina's soul. Then Lacey smiled, her face taking on a soft expression that spoke beyond her years. She held out her hand. "It'll be okay. I'll be with you."

Christina solemnly took her new friend's hand. Ben rolled his eyes.

As they walked down the hall, Ben leading, Christina wondered how a six-year-old could understand her better than her own fiancé.

CHAPTER 5

Ruth bustled about the noisy kitchen, getting out flour and other ingredients for the biscuits. But her mind lingered on Christina. Meeting everyone had gone okay, hadn't it? Christina was a beautiful girl. Ben was clearly proud of her.

All right now, Ruthie, stop. Time to think about supper.

Sy and the men would grill the ribs outside. But there was still corn on the cob to fix, and buttermilk biscuits, and fried potatoes with onions and mushrooms—a Dearing favorite. Ruth had made two apple pies early that morning. She took them out of the refrigerator to start warming, thinking she'd stick them in a low oven when they sat down to eat.

Maddy was slicing the potatoes, and Jess was setting the dining room table. Ruth could hear the plates and silverware clinking.

"What do you want me to do, Mama?" Sarah asked.

"Start shuckin' the corn."

Christina hung at the outskirts of the kitchen, close to the nearest family room chair, in which Ben sat. Lacey had been her constant companion for the last hour but had now drifted off toward the play room with Alex and Pogey. Penny had trotted after them. Ben was already in a bantering discussion with Sy, Don, and Jake about the golf game he'd missed. "Yeah, well, we're goin' back out tomorrow." Ben sounded so sure of himself. "And none of y'all's winnin' now that I'm here."

Ruth smiled at Christina. Girl looked like she didn't quite know what to do with herself, bless her heart. Although she was clearly trying to hide her discomfort. "Is there something I can do, Mrs. Dearing?" she asked.

"Oh, mercy, don't call me that." Ruth grinned. "You make me sound so old." At sixty-one, she probably did look ancient to Christina. "Just call me Mama Ruth. That's what a lot of people do."

Christina nodded, her palms rubbing against each other.

Ruth pointed toward the refrigerator. "Anyway, how 'bout cuttin' some onions? I keep 'em in the fridge so they won't make your eyes water. Maddy will show you what size we need."

"Okay."

Two plates clinked loudly in the dining room. Ruth called toward the sound. "Jess, what're you doin' in there, settin' my plates or breakin' 'em?"

"Breakin' 'em. Four down, eight to go."

Smart aleck.

36

Ruth turned back to the bag of flour on the counter. *Oh, wait.* "Jess." She spoke over her shoulder. "You need to set an extra plate. Tamel's comin'."

Maddy snickered. "Oh, boy."

Silence in the dining room. Then—*"What?"*

Ruth reached in a drawer for the measuring cup. "He wanted to come so I said sure."

Jess appeared in the doorway, hands full of silverware. "So you invited him, just like that? Just 'cause he wanted to come?"

"Why not? He's a good friend of yours, has been since grade school."

"We are *not* friends."

"What? Of course you are. He thinks you hung the moon."

"Apparently not anymore. And I don't think too much of him either."

Oh, dear. Ruth could guess what this was about. Christina kept her head down, cutting onions.

"Tamel Curd's comin' for diiiinner!" Ben singsonged. He looked to Christina. "He's Jess's boyfriend."

"Will you quit with that?" Jess pointed silverware at her brother. "He is *not* my boyfriend! I don't even *like* him."

Maddy reached for another potato. "Methinks the lady doth protest too much."

Sarah laughed.

"And furthermore, I *do not* want him here tonight." Jess glowered.

"Miss I-don't-need-a-man-in-my-life." Maddy muttered to the potato.

Jess threw her a look to kill.

37

Ruth faced her youngest daughter. "Come on now, Jess, you haven't seen Tamel since you were down for Easter."

"So?"

Jess lived only about four hours away in Memphis, but she worked so many hours in that law firm she hardly ever had a full weekend off to drive home. "What am I supposed to do? I've already invited him."

"So uninvite him."

"I'm not goin' to do that."

Jess snorted. "Stupid Camel T—"

"*Stop* callin' him that." Poor Tamel. He'd been teased unmercifully all through school because of his name. He certainly didn't need Jessica teasing him now.

Jess huffed. "I can't even come into town without him honin' in on the family."

"He's practically part of the family."

"No. He's. Not!"

Jess turned on her heel back into the dining room. The dishes clinked louder.

"Don't you break my plates!"

Sarah chuckled. "She's likely to throw 'em all across the room now."

Ruth glanced at Christina. The young woman was cutting onions as if her life depended on it. What must she think of Jess's tirade? Being so new to the family and all, she might wonder if they'd talk about *her* like that when she wasn't around.

"Don't you mind Jess." Ruth kept her tone mild as she measured flour. "She and Tamel grew up together—"

"They dated some in high school," Maddy put in. "But Jess'll never admit to it."

"We did *not* date!" Jess called from the dining room. "He just chased me all over tarnation is all."

"Oh, yeah? Did you or did you not go to the prom with him? That same year you tried to hem your dress?"

No answer.

"As I was sayin'"—Maddy turned to Christina—"they dated some in high school—"

"Goin' to the prom once is *not* datin'." Jess was in the doorway again, her face red. "And I only went with him 'cause my real date got sick at the last minute." She pivoted and stomped back to her work.

"Then they both went off to different colleges and law schools." Maddy didn't miss a beat in her slicing. "Now Tamel's back livin' in Justus. Took over his father's funeral home business—the only one in town. You die, you go see Tamel."

That bit of information pulled Christina's head up. She looked from Maddy to Ruth, as if wondering if she was being strung along.

"It's true." Ben sidled up to her. "Curd Funeral Home." He laughed. "Doesn't sound so appealin', huh."

"Yeah," Jess called, "it's even worse if you call him Camel Tu—."

"For heaven's sake, stop callin' him that." Ruth reached for the salt. "One of these days you're gonna slip up and say it to his face."

"Good. Maybe he'll quit comin' around."

Christina's knife still hung in the air. She gazed questioningly from Ben to Ruth. Tiny drops of moisture stood out on her forehead.

Oh, dear, poor thing. They were overwhelming her. Ruth shot Christina an encouraging smile.

"And really." Jess stalked back into the kitchen, her chore in the dining room done. "A funeral home? When he has a law degree and passed the bar? What a total waste of three years, not to mention a ton of money."

Sy got up from his chair. "It's his father's business, Jess. Henry's sick. He needed his son to come home. Surely you can understand that."

Jess just shook her head, a sound rattling in her throat. "Well, good for him. Hope he's happy haulin' corpses."

Don and Jake laughed.

"So did you set a plate for him?" Ruth looked her daughter in the eye.

"Yes, mother." Jess sounded none too happy about it.

"Good." Ben dipped his chin. "We'll make sure he sits next to you."

"Yeah." Don slapped his hands on his knees and stood. His blue eyes twinkled. "He'll be all over Jess like white on rice."

Jess flicked a look at the ceiling, her hands planting on her hips. "Honestly, y'all." She stalked through the family room and disappeared down the hall.

Ruth glanced at Christina and stilled. The young woman's face had paled.

Ben patted her on the shoulder. "It's okay, babe, everybody's just teasin'." His voice held that same lightheartedness Ruth had heard over the phone.

Christina gazed at him, as if trying to believe it was true.

"He's right." Ruth's hands were messy from mixing dough. She rested them on the sides of the glass bowl. "This family's always carryin' on. Shows we love each other."

Christina's eyes slid to Ruth. She tried to smile, but it came out shaky. Pressing her lips together, she bent her head over the onions and concentrated on chopping.

Goodness. Even Ruth hadn't expected her to be that sensitive.

"There, done!" Maddy put down her knife. A huge bowl of sliced potatoes sat before her.

"I'm thirsty," Ben said to no one in particular. "Whatcha got to drink around here?"

"Go sit down, Ben, I'll get it for you." Maddy moved to the sink to wash her hands.

"That's what I like — a woman who waits on me." Ben winked at Christina and moved toward the family room.

Christina didn't seem to like the comment. Ruth watched as her eyes followed Maddy's movements — pulling a Dr. Pepper out of the fridge, pouring it into a glass. Maddy presented it to Ben.

"Thank you, dear sister."

"You're welcome."

Christina turned back to the counter and stared at the cutting board, frowning. After a moment she bit her lip, then went back to cutting.

Now what? Ruth glanced at Ben. He took a drink of the Dr. Pepper and smacked his lips, oblivious to Christina's reaction. A cold dread rolled through Ruth's stomach. Things weren't going well here, but Ben was so much in love he couldn't see it.

Ruth shot a silent prayer to heaven. *Please, Lord, help us through this reunion — without my Ben's heart gettin' broken again.*

CHAPTER 6

Jess slid lipstick over her mouth, puckered her lips, then checked her face in her bedroom mirror. There. She looked great, if she did say so herself. This summer's tan was just the right toasty color.

She sighed and looked into her own green eyes. "Stupid Camel."

With a flip of her blonde hair she turned on her heel to leave the bedroom. She needed to get back into the kitchen and help with supper.

The minute she stepped into the hallway the noise and smells hit her, all the way from the kitchen. Someone must have opened the sliding glass door to the backyard. The ribs' tangy-sweet barbeque scent filtered into the house. The potatoes and corn and all were cooking in the kitchen, Mama's and her sister's voices chattering over each other. In the family room Don and Jake were deep in some never-ending discussion about everything that was wrong with politicians these days. Did those two men ever shut up? She sure was glad she had a room to herself, no husband yakkin' like that.

"Aunt Jess!" Alex's high little voice called from the living room, at the front of the house.

"What?" Jess stopped at the end of the hall.

"Tamel's here!"

Oh, spiffy.

"Wow, he's got a big yellow car!"

Jess cast an annoyed look toward the entryway. What in the world was Camel driving now? Last time she'd seen him, it was an old black VW bug. Guy had absolutely no taste.

Muttering under her breath, she headed toward the door.

The bell rang. Alex bounded to her side as Jess opened the door. Hot, humid air filtered into the house.

"Hi, beautiful." Tamel offered her a smile big enough to ratchet up both dimples. His sandy hair looked like it had just been cut. And those brown eyes of his looked as full of mischief as ever.

"Hey." Jess caught sight of a yellow apparition parked at the curb. She pushed Tamel to one side to get a better look. Then wished she hadn't. She gaped at the thing. "Where in the world did you get *that*?"

"Wow." Alex ran outside and down the porch steps for a closer look.

Tamel grinned. "Like it?"

"*Like* it? It's a banana-yellow *hearse*, for heaven's sake. How could anybody in their right mind like it?"

He cocked his head. "I think she's a beauty. I call her Chiquita."

"How original."

44

"Chiqui for short."

Jess gave him a look.

"Holds lots of luggage."

"Hm. If you're travelin' to a funeral."

Tamel mouthed a *ho-ho*. "Wanna go for a ride?"

"Tamel Curd, I wouldn't be caught dead in that thing."

He raised his hands. "Yeah, well, a lot of people were, you know."

"Oh, great, that *really* makes me want to get inside."

"At least I painted it yellow. I figured black was just too depressin'."

"So you took an old hearse from the family business, and now you're drivin' it for fun?"

"Yeah. It was Dad's oldest. And my old Bug had about had it, so I figured this would do me good."

Do me good. What kind of talk was that for a man who'd passed the bar? He sounded like a hick.

Tamel eyed Jess, that teasing little smile playing around his mouth. *So* annoying.

Alex had opened the rear door of the yellow hearse and was crawling around the back. "Alex!" Jess folded her arms. "Get out of there!" No telling what germs were still around inside.

Alex stuck her face out of the beast. "I wanna go for a ride with Lacey!"

Tamel glanced sideways at Jess as if to say *See?* "Later, Rugrat. It's probably 'bout time for supper."

Frowning, Alex slipped out of the car and banged the door shut.

"Hey, you don't have to close it so hard," Tamel called. "You might wake the dead." He looked at Jess, then burst out laughing.

Jess rolled her eyes.

45

They waited for a pouting Alex, then headed for the family room. At which point the noise level only grew. Everyone had to greet Tamel with such effusion, as if they really liked the guy. Pogey's and Lacey's eyes lit up at the mere sight of him. Alex bounced on the balls of her feet. "You should see his car!"

So naturally everybody had to pile outside and take a gander at the ugly thing. They all thought it was hilarious. "No commitin' a crime in that," Dad said. "The police would beat feet to your door."

"I don't know, it sets me to coffin." Don held a fist to his mouth and faked a hack.

"Yeah, pretty grave sight." Jake shook his head solemnly.

Oh, good grief.

Ben hung off to the side, his arm around Christina. When Ben got the chance in all the hubbub to introduce his fiancée to Tamel, what did the guy do? Took her hand and kissed it, like some knight in shining armor. "What a beautiful addition to the family."

Christina looked taken aback, then gave him a warm smile.

Terrific. He'd brainwashed even her.

"All right, time to get supper on the table." Mama turned toward the house. "Sy, are the ribs done?"

"To perfection, my love."

Tamel rubbed his palms together. "Oh, boy, the Dearings' cookin'. Can't wait."

Tamel's mama had died when he was ten. Henry Curd never was much of a cook. Nor a father, either, for that matter. They pretty much lived on frozen dinners and macaroni. Except, of course, whenever Tamel could get himself invited to the Dearings'.

Which was often. Once in a while Mama convinced Henry to come too. The man just sort of dried up when he lost his wife. He threw himself into his funeral home business, and it grew—until people from surrounding small towns came to him in their time of grief.

Mama smiled at Tamel. "Sorry your dad couldn't come."

"Yeah. You know how he is. Besides, he's not feelin' all that well these days. He works a few hours a day, then needs to rest."

"Oh, I'm so sorry to hear that."

Henry was only sixty-six, but years of smoking had taken their toll. He had bad lungs and a bad heart. All-around bad combination.

Mama patted Tamel on the shoulder, then headed up the steps. "All right, family, let's eat."

"Yeah." Maddy prodded her daughter, Alex, toward the house. "Let's get this meal on the road."

Sarah guffawed. "On the road, Maddy?"

Jess poked Sarah in the shoulder. "Doesn't she mean 'get this show on the table?'"

They both laughed loudly.

Maddy raised both hands—*I give up.*

Still giggling, Sarah prodded Pogey to pick up his shoes from the lawn. "They're dry now. And wash your feet for supper."

"I just did wash 'em!" Pogey's chubby cheeks were red with the heat.

"That was three hours ago. Do it again."

"Man." Pogey stomped across the yard, shoulders rounded.

Jess caught Christina's eye and shrugged as if to say *The joys of family.* Christina smiled back. Tentatively, but a smile all the same.

47

Well. That was something.

It took another fifteen minutes for glasses to be filled with sweet tea, and the long dining table to be loaded with caramel-red ribs, corn on the cob, Mama's biscuits and homemade jam, and the mouthwatering fried potatoes and onions. Mama did her typical table check to see if she'd forgotten anything. Her eyebrows rose. "Maddy, fetch a jar of pickled watermelon rind from the fridge. Then we're ready."

Lady Penelope withdrew to the family room couch, where she sat watching the goings-on. Jess walked over to pet her. "Yeah, you know what's comin', don't you."

Penny held her head high, as if to say *Fine by me, I need some alone time anyway.*

"All right, come on, Jess, we're ready." Mama's face looked flushed.

Jess pointed a finger at Penny. "Okay, family's eatin'."

Penny gave her a disdainful look — *I'm on the couch, what more do you want?*

"Go on now."

It had been Dad's rule since they'd gotten Penny. No canines at the table. To make sure she stayed away, the Yorkie had to retreat to her bed and could not get up until the meal was done.

With a martyred sigh, Lady Penelope jumped off the couch and headed to her bed. She fussed around in circles three times, then flopped down with her back to Jess.

In the dining room everybody crowded around the table, ready to take their regular seats, Mama and Dad on each end, and the kids near their mothers. But Lacey insisted on sitting next to Christina, which threw off the balance, so Sarah's and Maddy's

48

families switched sides. Ben sat on the other side of Christina, who was across from Jess. And—of course—Tamel ended up next to Jess. Terrific. He gallantly pulled back her chair. She allowed him a smile. "Thank you."

He threw her a *you-know-you-like-me* look.

Uh-huh.

Christina leaned into Ben's shoulder, and he gave her a wink. Girl looked all tight-muscled, as much she tried to hide it. Jess felt the waves rolling off her. Ben didn't seem to notice in the least. All he could do was beam that sloppy *I'm-so-in-love* grin around the table. Thing about Ben was, he had the biggest heart. And when he was happy, he just assumed everyone else in the world was happy with him.

Well. Nothing like throwing Christina into the fire. If she survived a Dearing supper, she could survive anything.

CHAPTER 7

Christina held Ben's hand under the table. Chairs stuttered across the carpet as everyone else got settled. Christina saw Mr. Dearing catch his wife's eye down the length of the table, then make a point of looking right and left. Lips curved, he gazed back at his wife and raised his eyebrows in a silent message. Whatever he meant, she understood perfectly. She gave him a smile so full of love it rattled Christina's heart.

Why did she have to feel so stupid around these people?

The whole family was nice, including Tamel, who was really friendly, not to mention hot. Even if Jess tried to pretend he wasn't. His face was amazing, and then there were those dimples. And he had this half smile most of the time, like he loved the world and the world loved him back. Kind of like Ben. Tamel and all the Dearings were so ... easy with each other. And with themselves. How did it feel to be like that? To be so confident in yourself?

"All right, let's pray." Mr. Dearing held out his hands, and everyone else did the same. Lacey's little fingers reached for Christina's. All heads bowed, including Ben's. Christina looked around the table, then quickly dropped her chin.

"Lord Jesus, thank you for bringin' all the family home and safe." Mr. Dearing's voice had a strong ring to it. "And special thanks for bringin' Christina to us. We ask your blessin' on this food and this conversation. Amen."

Amens repeated around the table.

There was so much to eat. And the food was incredible. Christina had never tasted ribs like Mr. Dearing's, even though she lived in Texas, known for its barbeque. All the dishes went around once, then a second time. The biscuits were melt-in-your-mouth. And the homemade jam was wonderful.

Christina could hardly keep up with the various conversations. Mrs. Dearing—Mama Ruth—asking Pogey about his school. Mr. Dearing and Tamel talking about the funeral home. Sarah was telling Maddy about some difficult client in her conference-planning business. Maddy talked about her work at the preschool Alex had attended.

"You still likin' retirement, Dad?" Ben asked. Christina knew Mr. Dearing had sold his Ford car dealership in Jackson early that year.

"Yup. Didn't think I would. But it's nice to get up and think, 'I don't have to work today. Maybe I'll just read. Or play golf.'"

"The life of Riley, huh." Ben grinned. "Sounds great. That'll be me in ... oh, forty years."

Sounded like forever.

"Oh, need to be takin' pictures." Jake scooted back from the table and picked up a camera lying on the sideboard. He moved around, clicking off shots. Everyone just kept on talking and eating, like it was no big deal. Christina kept her head down.

"Come on, Christina, look up."

Heat sizzled through her nerves. She hated pictures of herself. Raising her chin, she tried to smile as the camera flashed.

"There, thanks." Jake nodded at her.

"Say, who's got the picture this year?" Mr. Dearing's voice boomed down the table.

"We do," Sarah said.

"Know what you're gonna do yet?"

"We're workin' on it." Jake sat down and picked up his fork.

Sarah shook her head. "We should have had this planned long ago. But Mr. Detail Man here just can't get it together."

Ben leaned over and whispered. "Sarah's not only a conference planner, she wants her total *life* planned out."

"I heard that." Sarah threw him a look.

Christina licked her lips. "What's 'the picture?'"

She meant the question for Ben, but it pinged around the table.

"Ben hasn't told you about our family calendars?" Maddy frowned at her brother. "Why haven't you shown them to her?"

Ben shrugged. "Hey, we've only been dating for ten weeks."

Jess raised an eyebrow, as if she knew that fact all too well. Christina focused on her plate.

53

"I'll tell you, Christina," Maddy said. "Every summer reunion we take a crazy photo of everybody together. Each family has their turn at figurin' out where the picture's gonna be taken. It can get pretty wild."

"Only because everybody tries to outdo each other," Ben put in.

Lacey grinned. "Last year Uncle Ben made us all climb a tree."

Mrs. Dearing raised both hands. "I'm not doin' that again."

Jess looked smug. "Mine was the best, and y'all know it. Even if we did have to go kinda far."

Tamel leaned forward toward Christina, as if sharing a secret. "Only because *I* gave her the idea."

"Shut up, Tamel." Jess elbowed him.

"You know it's true."

Christina looked questioningly from Tamel to Jess.

"We were sittin' in pink bathtubs!" Alex burst out a high, loud giggle.

Bathtubs?

"Oh, ha, look at her face." Don gestured toward Christina.

"Oh, y'all, now hush." Jess waved her hand around. "We went to a Habitat for Humanity Restore in Jackson, about thirty-five minutes away. They had three big bathtubs, all pink, can you believe it—"

"Lacey and me were in the same one!" Alex's pixie face lit up.

Jess nodded. "This guy who works there knows Tamel, so he let us get in the tubs. We all crammed in like sausages, and he took the pictures for us."

Christina smiled. Sounded crazy but fun. "Does everyone get a copy?"

"You bet." Jess waved a hand, nearly knocking over her glass of tea. "Every year I make a calendar with pictures of our reunions for each family. I've got my calendars goin' years back. Great memories, lookin' through 'em."

What a fun idea. And to have memories worth thinking about ... "I'll bet."

Things got quiet for about half a second. Then conversations started up around different parts of the table. More food was passed, and everyone kept eating. Christina chewed on the ribs, but her mind hung up on Jess's words. Calendars and memories. People you *wanted* to be with. Her heart surged. She had to make this work. Not just survive the reunion and hurry back home. But really become a part of the family.

Jess was watching her, as if trying to figure out what she was thinking. "So, Ben tells me you work as an admin at the company?"

"Yes."

"How long have you been there?"

"I just started three months ago."

"Oh. So Ben and you two met pretty soon after that."

All other conversation died away. Suddenly everyone was looking at Christina.

"Mm-hm. A couple of weeks."

"The first time I saw her I flipped." Ben picked up his glass of tea. "Took me two days to get up the courage to ask her out. I figured everybody would be hittin' on her."

Christina blinked at him. Get up the courage? She couldn't begin to imagine laid-back Ben short on self-confidence.

"Was everybody?" Jess asked.

Yeah, right. "No." Christina shrugged. "I just kinda kept my head down. It was a new job, and I had a lot to learn."

Mama Ruth picked up the plate of corn and sent it around again. Not many ears left in the huge bowl. "Tell us about your family, Christina. I hear you're the only child?"

Christina stiffened. Here it came. The questions. She pinned on a pleasant expression. "Yes."

An awkward, roaring silence followed. Christina racked her brain for something else to say.

"How about your mom and dad? Do they live near you?"

For a nano-second Christina had a wild urge to spit out the truth—all of it—and get it over with.

"My father died last year."

Christina felt Ben stiffen beside her. He exchanged a surprised look with Jess across the table. Panic spritzed through Christina's veins. Oh, no. She hadn't told him that, had she. She'd acted like they were both still alive ...

"Oh, I'm so sorry." Mama Ruth sounded genuinely sad. "He must have died at a young age."

Christina's heart banged around. Ben couldn't stand being lied to, he'd told her that. "Fifty-one." She didn't dare glance at Ben.

Mama Ruth looked stricken. Christina knew she was ten years older than that herself.

"Is your mother in good health?"

Good enough to chase after every man she saw, even at fifty years old. At least that's all she talked about whenever she called. "Yes."

"Does she live close to you?"

Never far enough. "She's in Austin."

"Oh. Well, that's not too far away to visit."

Christina managed a nod.

More awkward silence.

Ben cleared his throat. Pointed to the potatoes. "Please pass those, Don."

He already had some on his plate.

The bowl started around. Ben watched its progress as if it might disappear any minute. Christina could feel his deep disappointment that she'd lied to him. Like a wall had suddenly gone up between them. Her hands started to shake. She hid them in her lap.

Everyone was looking at her. They knew, didn't they. That she had so much to hide.

The seconds trailed out. Christina felt her face go hot.

"So, Tamel." Maddy's voice was over-light. She had to lean around Jess to see his face. "What's new in your life?"

The focus shifted to him. But Christina felt little relief. Her insides still trembled. With effort, she picked up her fork.

Tamel scratched his cheek. "Well, I did have quite the situation a few weeks ago."

"Oh, do tell."

Most everyone perked up, expectation on their faces. Jess shook her head, as if already bored. Ben shoved food in his mouth, inches—and a world— away from Christina.

Tamel laid down his fork and knife. "Well, you know I moved in with Dad about ten months ago. And those crazy neighbors next to him—the Berkenshires?—they've got these pet rabbits in a bunch of cages. Drives Rufus nuts." Tamel looked across the table at Christina. "Rufus is my dad's hound dog."

She managed a nod. Her throat felt so dry. She took a drink of tea.

"I don't know who procreates more, the Berkenshires or the rabbits. The last five years every time I came home they had another kid. And the rabbit cages keep gettin' bigger. Rufus knows he's not supposed to go in that yard, but the pull is just too strong. He slinks down there at night and noses around the cages. Just imagine all those tasty treats sittin' in front of you, and no way to get to 'em."

Jess reached for another rib, trying to look uninterested.

"One night a couple weeks ago Burt Berkenshire—that's the dad—comes up to my door with a shotgun. Says he sees my dog in his yard one more time, he's gonna pull the trigger."

Mrs. Dearing gasped. "He wouldn't do that!"

Christina felt numb. What would happen when Ben demanded to know why she hadn't told him her father was dead?

"Oh, yes, he would." Tamel's head went up and down. "So I started puttin' Rufus in the garage at night. Crazy dog howls around and lets me know he's mighty unhappy. I told him it's all his fault 'cause he wouldn't behave himself. Anyway, three nights ago he got out. I think Dad left the backdoor not totally latched. I didn't know it till the next mornin' when Rufus shows up on my porch with a dead, dirty rabbit in his mouth."

Oh-nos and laughter flew around the table. Christina forced a laugh, too—then wished she hadn't. It sounded so fake.

Ben kept eating.

Lacey gripped Christina's leg. "Did that man kill Rufus?"

"No, Little Lace, don't you worry," Tamel said.

"Did you hide his gun, Uncle Tamel?"

"Nope. I hid the dead rabbit. Sort of."

"You must have buried it." Mr. Dearing's eyebrows raised.

Tamel dipped his chin. "Tell you the truth, I panicked when I saw that dead critter. Usually I'd do the honest thing and go over to my neighbor's and admit what happened. But I couldn't and have Rufus live to see another sunrise. Besides, it wasn't totally my dog's fault. He got outta the garage, sure, but who let that rabbit outta its cage? So I did the only thing I could think of. I cleaned up that dead-as-a-doornail rabbit and snuck over to the Berkenshire's yard that night." Tamel hunched his shoulders. "My heart liked to beat outta my ribs. If Burt woke up, *I'd* be the dead one instead of Rufus. But I managed to stuff that critter back in his cage without makin' a sound. Then I hightailed it home."

Mr. and Mrs. Dearing exchanged grins. Even Ben chuckled. Hope trickled through Christina. *Please, God, please ...*

Maddy tilted her head. "Tamel Curd, I never thought I'd live to see you so devious."

He shrugged — *what else could I do?*

Jake laughed. "Ol' Burt musta thought that rabbit had a sudden heart attack."

Tamel picked up his fork, then put it back down. "Actually, it wasn't that simple." He scratched his chin. "See, the next day I got up and went outside. Couldn't help lookin' over at their yard, wonderin' when somebody would find the dead rabbit. They say a criminal returns to the scene of the crime. Guess so. I was just hopin' it wasn't one of the kids that found the rabbit. So what do I see but Burt Berkenshire standin' in front of the deadie's cage. And he stands there and stands there. The man just doesn't move. I'm startin' to get more and more antsy, thinkin' *what?* Did I leave my DNA all over the corpse or somethin'?"

The laughter grew louder. Christina glanced at Jess. She was leaning on her elbow away from Tamel, looking at him as if she didn't believe a word he said.

"So finally I can't stand it anymore. I call out, 'Hey, Burt! Everything okay with your rabbits?' He turns around and looks at me, all pale-faced. Like he's seen a ghost. So I say, 'What's wrong?' and start walkin' over to him." Tamel listed toward Jess. "You know, the criminal actin' all innocent."

She flicked a look at the ceiling.

"When I get up to Burt, all he can do is point toward the cage. And there lies the dead rabbit, just like I left him. Then Burt looks at me, all jittery, and says, 'That ol' hare died yesterday. I buried him way out in the field, where the kids wouldn't find him. Now here he is again, all cleaned up.'" Tamel widened his eyes and raised both hands, fingers curved. "'Back from the graaaaave!'"

Laughter burst around the table. Ben chuckled, but it sounded stiff. Mr. Dearing pounded his fist, making his plate jump. Mama Ruth laughed so hard her eyes filled with tears. The sounds washed through Christina but could not clear her lungs.

Jess just crossed her arms.

"Ah, come on." Tamel poked her shoulder. "You know that's funny."

"What I know is it's not true."

"Is so."

"Is not. I've *heard* that story before, passed around on the Internet. You go to Snopes, you'll see it's made up."

Tamel's forehead wrinkled. "Snopes?"

"Snopes.com, where you go to see if some story forwarded in e-mails is true or not."

Tamel's jaw dropped. "Snopes is tellin' *my* story?"

"Yes, Tamel." Jess's head wagged. "For years now."

Indignation flattened Tamel's face. "How can that be? This just happened two weeks ago!"

Jess picked up her glass of sweet tea. "Uh-huh."

Christina stole a glance at Ben. His eyes flicked to her, then back to Tamel.

Mama Ruth wiped a tear from her eye. "Well, I think it's true. I've never known Tamel to make up stories."

"Me too," Lacey declared.

Pogey's round face was split with a grin. "Whatja do after he told you that, Uncle Tamel?"

Tamel chuckled. "I just backed away real slow, like I didn't want any part of a ghost rabbit. I did manage to say 'Sorry for your loss.'"

That sent everyone laughing again. Jess rolled her eyes.

Slowly the table quieted. Silverware clinked. The family turned their attention once again to the food. Christina didn't want to eat another thing. She picked up her fork and forced down a bite of meat.

Ben drank the last of his tea and set down his empty glass. In a heartbeat Jess was up to refill it. Christina's eyes tracked her into the kitchen and back, carrying the pitcher. Jess refilled Ben's glass, then others'. Ben didn't even say thank you.

61

The dread in Christina's stomach deepened. Would he expect her to wait on him like that? Just like she'd had to wait on her father?

"Uh-oh." Mr. Dearing's amused voice jerked Christina from her thoughts. She looked up to see him gesturing with his chin toward the doorway into the kitchen. At the threshold close to the floor a little golden snout and one eye peeked around the corner.

"Aw." Jess made an empathetic sound in her throat. "We're takin' too long."

"What else is new?" Mrs. Dearing laughed.

"Lady Penelope." Mr. Dearing's tone pulsed with authority. But there was love in it, too, not meanness. "We're still eatin'."

The nose disappeared. From around the corner came a loud and long doggie sigh. Little toenails slowly clicked across the tiled kitchen floor.

Mr. Dearing shook his head at Christina. Could he tell how on the edge she was? "She gets impatient."

Christina swallowed. She needed to say *something.* "Will she go back to her bed?"

"Yup. But you wait, the minute she hears people gettin' up, she'll be out here."

The rest of the meal blurred. People talked and laughed and ate. Christina put food in her mouth and shoved it down, no longer tasting. Ben felt like a block of ice next to her.

Finally Mrs. Dearing and her three daughters got up to clear the table. Christina rose to help. When they entered the kitchen, bearing plates, Penny bounced out of her bed. Maddy pointed and told her to get back. "We're not done yet."

The Yorkie walked away on stiff legs, nose held high, as if to say *"I don't need you anyway."*

62

Jess stifled a laugh. "She only puts on that air when there's people around to see her. When we're in the dinin' room it's the big ol' sigh. She doesn't seem to realize we can hear her."

Jess was trying to be nice. Act like she didn't see what was going on between Christina and Ben. Christina glanced back into the dining room and caught his eye. He looked away.

Her heart folded over.

Mrs. Dearing pulled two warmed apple pies from the oven. Maddy fetched a large plastic container from the fridge. Whipped cream.

"I'll make the coffee." Sarah moved toward the large coffee maker.

"Oh, no, you won't." Maddy used a hip to nudge her sister aside.

"But I brought my own grind!"

"You always bring your own, you coffee snob. That doesn't mean the rest of us want to drink that motor oil."

"Now, girls." Mama Ruth spoke mildly, as if she'd heard this argument before.

"*Motor* oil?" Sarah ran a hand through her short brown hair. "I'll have you know it's expensive coffee, ground to perfection."

"It's not the brand." Maddy poured water into the machine. "It's just that you make it so doggone strong."

Christina leaned against the counter, trying to disappear.

"Oh, humph." Sarah made a face. "You can put water in yours, but I can't make mine stronger."

"So make yourself one of your lattes, and let me make the coffee for everyone else."

Sarah stuck her hands on her hips. "Fine, then. Think I will." She looked to Christina. "You like lattes?"

Christina's nerves pinged. The last thing she needed right now was to be stuck in an argument between Ben's sisters. She glanced from Sarah to Maddy. "I guess."

Sarah lowered her chin at the wishy-washy answer. "Do you like lattes, or don't you?"

Christina swallowed. She glanced around for Mrs. Dearing, but the woman was back in the dining room. Jess stood across the kitchen, watching Christina. "I ... yes."

Sarah shot a satisfied smile at Maddy. "So would you like one tonight? I'll make you the greatest one you've ever had."

As if her stomach could take another thing—

"Don't listen to her, Christina." Jess wagged a finger. "That drink will be so thick it could walk down the street. And it'll keep you up all night."

Sarah narrowed her eyes at her sister. "Excuse me, Jessica, but you are not in this conversation. And besides, it's decaf."

Jess and Sarah eyed each other, then turned to Christina—*well?*

Christina licked her lips. "I ... sure, I'd love one."

"Hah, see there?" Sarah waved a hand at her sisters. "Christina, my dear, you will not be sorry."

A unison response from Maddy and Jess—"Yes, you will."

Mrs. Dearing returned, carrying small plates from the dining hutch. Christina helped her put slices on the plates and take them out to the table. When Christina placed a piece before Ben, she dared to touch his shoulder. He looked up at her and blinked, no smile. His expression mixed anger and hurt.

She'd *hurt* him? The thought pierced her to the core. And almost frightened her more than his anger. How would he act when he was alone with her? Would he hit her?

Christina gave him a shaky smile and turned back to the kitchen.

"Y'all go ahead and eat," Sarah called to her family. "Christina and I are makin' lattes."

"Weren't waitin' for ya anyway," Jess said. But Christina heard a smile wrapped around the words.

Relief struck Christina in the chest. One quiet moment. She leaned against the counter, feeling weak. Her tired eyes followed Sarah's movements in the latte-making process.

Sarah had a way about her that seemed so ... definitive. Like she knew every step and followed each one precisely. Sarah had a pretty face. Strong jawline and clear, milky skin. Not tanned like Jess or Maddy. She certainly didn't look nearly forty.

Sarah measured milk and half-and-half into a cup. "So when's the wedding?"

Christina blinked. "I ... we don't know. Things have all happened so fast ..."

Probably wouldn't be one now.

"No time to talk about it?"

"Something like that."

Sarah poured the creamy contents into two mugs. "Well, don't worry. When the time's right, it'll happen."

"Yeah." The response sounded weak to her own ears.

"Ben sure seems happy." Sarah pushed the dairy cartons aside.

65

Christina searched her face. Was he really? She'd assumed he was always like that. "Well. Good."

Sarah glanced at her and smiled.

Laughter erupted from the dining room. Jess's voice rose in some comment, followed by a retort from Tamel. Exhaustion trailed through Christina. She did not want to go back in there. Her mouth was tired from fake smiles. And surely everyone could see her heart beat through her shirt.

Could she do this for the rest of her life? Was this really what she wanted?

Sarah began to froth the milk. No need to try to talk above the gurgling. Christina fought to beat back her emotions before they had to join the rest of the family.

When the frothing was done Sarah brewed the coffee, then poured it into the milk. "Here you go."

"Thanks." Christina stared at the mug.

"Well go ahead, try it."

Christina lifted the mug and took a tentative sip. The drink slid down her throat, strong and creamy. *Good.* Her eyes widened. "It's wonderful."

Sarah's lips curved. "Don't sound so surprised."

"I didn't mean —"

She raised a hand. "Christina. Relax." She looked deep into Christina's eyes, as if she saw right through her.

Christina looked away. Managed a small nod.

Sarah sighed with satisfaction. "Yippee. I get to go in there and announce to my sisters I have a new coffee buddy."

Did that mean Jess and Maddy wouldn't like her now? If they'd ever liked her at all.

66

Christina sipped her latte while Sarah made her own drink. With every swallow the coffee tasted better. But her insides felt hollow.

"You don't have to stay in here with me, Christina. Go eat your pie."

"That's okay. I want to."

A minute passed in silence as Sarah frothed milk. When she was done Christina dared to ask a question. "I saw something when we all first sat down at the table. Mr. Dearing looked at Mrs.— Mama Ruth—and then looked all around, then back at her. I just wondered ... it sort of felt like they'd done it a hundred times."

Sarah smiled. "You picked that up, huh. Daddy's done that as long as I can remember."

"What's it mean?"

"It means he's looked around the room and seen that she's the prettiest one there."

The words hit Christina in the chest. A husband would do that? After all those years of marriage?

Sarah clicked the espresso machine dial over to brew the coffee. "He always tells us girls we're beautiful too. But we know Mama holds that special place in his heart. He started it years ago, when they were datin'. At first after lookin' around, he'd say the words—'you're the prettiest one here.' But after awhile they didn't need the words anymore."

Christina turned the last sentence over in her mind. What must it feel like to be that close to someone? To love each other so much you didn't need words ...

The coffee finished brewing. Sarah poured it and the milk into her mug. "All right, done. Let's go sit down."

Ben materialized in the kitchen doorway, carrying his empty dessert plate. His gaze latched onto Christina's. Sarah's eyes moved from her brother to Christina and back. "Excuse me, Ben." She edged past him into the dining room.

With a sigh, he crossed the kitchen and set his plate in the sink. He turned to Christina. "I think we'd better talk. Let's take a drive."

She nodded, numb.

CHAPTER 8

Ben opened the door of his car for Christina. She was looking like a scared rabbit. What was she expecting him to do, hit her or something? She slid inside, head down.

He got in and started the engine. It was stuffy hot in the car. He punched the air conditioner on high. No way could they talk anywhere near the house. Even now he could practically feel the eyes of his whole family watching out the window. Even if they weren't. Even if they were sitting around the table, laughing, pretending they didn't notice anything wrong—when everything was.

Ben's lungs burned. How did things go wrong so fast? Sure, Chris had been evasive about her family, but to not tell him her dad was dead? And he'd specifically *asked* about her parents. Oh, that look in Jess's eye when she realized he hadn't known. After he'd told her up and down how everything between him and Chris was so good. His sister could always see right through him. She knew he couldn't stand anyone to lie to him.

He backed out of the driveway and headed up the road, away from town.

Chris focused out her window.

They drove a mile in silence. An old dirt road came up on the right. Ben turned into it and put the car in Park.

He turned toward his fiancée. With obvious reluctance, she faced him.

"So." He kept his voice even. "I'm really sorry your father is dead. I'm also really sorry you didn't tell me. In fact, you led me to believe he was alive."

Silence.

"*Why?*"

"I didn't mean to."

"Didn't mean to what? Lie to me?"

"I didn't lie."

"Then what would you call it?"

Christina licked her lips. "I just ... when you asked, I didn't want to talk about it."

"Well, *I* want to talk about it. Now."

Part of Ben felt like a heel. This was about a dead parent. He should be consoling instead of confronting. Not that Christina seemed to care her father was gone.

Christina lifted a hand. "There's not much to tell. I wasn't living with them. I moved out when I was eighteen. I told you that."

Barely. She hadn't told him why. It's not like she'd gone off to college. So why not stay at home a few more years and save some rent money?

70

Ben shut his eyes. Tried to gentle his voice. "How did your father die?"

Christina looked out the windshield. "Heart attack, I think."

What was this? She didn't *know?*

He put his finger beneath her chin. Urged her to face him. "Look at me."

Slowly her eyes met his.

"What aren't you tellin' me?"

Christina pulled back and folded her arms. "I don't like talking about my parents."

"Why?"

"Because I ... just don't."

"That's not good enough. I need to *know* you. Understand you. And all the sudden I realize you're purposely keeping things from me. Which means you don't trust me."

She stared out the windshield.

"You know what that feels like, you lyin' to me? It means I'm not important enough to you to trust."

"I trust you."

"Then why won't you open up to me?"

Her chin dropped. "Can't we do this later?"

Was she that clueless? "Later? Like when? After we're married?"

Her fingers curled inward. She shook her head.

"Okay then. I'm listening."

Christina wouldn't raise her chin. Frustration and empathy surged through Ben. He wanted to shake her. He wanted to hold her and tell her everything would be okay.

"Christina. Please. Tell me about your parents."

Silence.

"Come *on!*"

71

She gave him a sudden, hard look. "They weren't nice, okay? Not like your perfect family." She glared at him.

"I never said my family was perfect. Heck, you've met 'em."

"Well, they're a whole lot better than mine."

And that was somehow *his* fault?

Ben focused on the steering wheel, working his jaw. Pulling his emotions back.

"Okay." He shifted in his seat. "That's a start. So ... what exactly did your parents do? And why is bein' with my family makin' you so uncomfortable?"

"It's not."

Ben blew out air. "Yes, it is! You haven't been normal since we got to the house! I've told everybody for days how wonderful you are, and then you get here and act like some whipped child."

Chris flinched.

"So start talkin' to me!"

She faced him, her mouth setting in a hard line. Something about her expression told Ben she'd crossed a Rubicon. Made a decision she'd been holding back. "Fine. If you really want to know."

"Of *course* I do."

She tilted her head, a defiant gesture. "My mother and father were both alcoholics. I can't remember a time when they loved me. Or didn't neglect and beat me. I've had five broken bones. Countless black eyes and bruises. My childhood was beyond awful. *Nobody* cared about me, nobody. The neighbors turned their backs. The church down the street didn't help. Social services didn't rescue me." She faced Ben, breathing heavily, tears glistening in her eyes. "I moved out the day I turned eighteen. Didn't talk to either of my parents for four years.

72

Then my dad died. I don't miss him. I still talk to my mom as little as possible. She's nothin' but a—"

Chris abruptly stopped, as if stunned at her own flow of words.

Ben stared at her, his insides gone cold. He'd figured she'd maybe had some kind of rough childhood, but *this*. "I'm so sorry." He could barely choke the words out.

She lowered her eyes, then gazed at him again, a tear falling on her cheek. The sight of it spun rage through Ben. Christina was so wonderful. He could imagine the beautiful child she'd been. How could her parents have treated her like that?

He reached for her and held her tightly. She started to cry hard, her shoulders shaking. Dark thoughts about her nasty parents trudged through Ben's mind. It was *good* her father was dead. As for the mother, they wouldn't need to have a thing to do with her.

No wonder Chris didn't know how to react to his family.

After some time she quieted and pulled away.

Ben kept hold of her hands. "Why was it so hard to tell me this?"

She looked past him, as if seeking an answer. Her face, so open a minute ago, seemed to shutter again. "I don't … it's hard to talk about."

Yeah, but they were planning to live the rest of their lives together.

"Do you feel ashamed or somethin'?"

She hesitated, then gave a tiny nod.

"Why? It wasn't your fault. It was your parents'."

Christina's mouth opened, then shut.

"You know that, right?"

73

For a long moment Ben waited. Heaviness bloomed in his chest—sadness for her pain. And disappointment that she wouldn't let him into her thoughts as he'd done with her. *"Right?"*

Slowly, her lips curved. "Yes. Sure."

Another lie. Ben could spot it now—that reticence in her face. A flat smile that didn't reach her eyes. Hadn't he seen the expression a dozen times before? It wasn't shyness. It was deceit.

The realization made him rethink every one of their conversations. All of them full of lies. The thought was more than he could bear.

"Chris, you really don't trust me. Because even now you're doing it. You're holding back. When I've never held back from you."

"No, I'm—"

"I want to help you." Ben cradled her face with his palms. "I want to make you forget your childhood. Build a new life. But I can't if you won't let me inside your *head.*"

"I will. I promise I will." Her words tinged with panic.

"Will isn't good enough. How about right *now*?"

"Okay." Her cheeks reddened, tension stiffening her body. "Please. I don't want to lose you."

Ben pulled his head back. "What? You're not going to lose me."

She gazed at him as if wanting so hard to believe that. Ben gazed back, his forehead crinkling. What was going on here?

Christina shut her eyes. Said nothing.

Ben took his hands from her face. What did he have to do, pull every bit out of her? "Okay." He leaned against his car door. "I'm going to ask you some questions. All I ask from you is the truth. No

74

hiding. None of that 'Sure, Ben, everything's great' when it obviously isn't. Okay?"

She nodded.

"Good. You know what your parents did was terrible, right?"

"Of course."

"Do you hate them for it?"

Christina hesitated. "Most of the time."

Ben eyed her. "Then why do you feel shame within yourself? I mean, I get that sometimes we can feel ashamed for something a family member does. But it seems to go deeper than that with you."

She looked at him for the longest time. Fresh tears welled in her eyes. When she finally spoke she choked out the words. "That's why this isn't going to work."

"What's *this?*"

"Us."

"What are you *talking* about?"

Her jaw tightened. "Because you have to *ask* me why I feel ashamed. You don't get it. You'll never get it."

Never? That wasn't fair. "So enlighten me."

Defiance returned to her eyes. "You've been built up all your life by parents who love you, Ben Dearing. Who've always said you could do anything. Who gave you confidence. Your past is what makes you *you.* The way you trust people, the way you see the world is all because of what you were taught in your childhood." Christina swiped at a tear. "How do you think you'd see the world if your parents always said you were worth nothing? That they were sorry you were born, because now they had to feed you?" Her voice hardened. "That you were ugly and insignificant and would never amount to anything."

Every word hit Ben in the chest. "I'm so sor—"

"I'm not through." Her hand shot up.

"Ok—"

"What if you dreaded to wake up every morning because you were afraid how you'd be treated? Or worse yet, you *knew*. What if the sound of your father's footsteps made you shake? What if you grew up knowing you couldn't trust anyone or anything? That life could end in a minute? And sometimes"— Christina's mouth trembled—"you wished it would."

"Chris—"

"What kind of person would you be today, huh, Ben?" Tears spilled down her cheeks. "You think you'd still be laid-back and easy? Confident? Think you'd just open up to people, believing they were going to love you—when no one else ever had?"

Ben's heart was about to break. "But I *do* love you."

"Because you don't know me!" Her voice rose. "Because you think I'm some perfect person who's going to fit into your perfect world!"

"I do know you, Chris. And what I don't know, I want to learn."

"Really? Then guess what—I *hate* being called Chris!"

Ben's eyebrows rose. "I'm sorry, I didn't know—"

"My father used to call me that. He'd never let me forget I was supposed to be a boy. My name's *Christina*."

"Okay, okay." Ben held up both palms in an *I-give*. "Christina. It's a pretty name, I like it."

He waited, afraid to say anything else wrong.

Christina regarded him, her jaw still set. Little by little her expression relaxed. Finally she blinked

76

away. "There." Now she sounded toneless. As if she'd just thrown her life away. "I told you."

No kidding. And there had to be more. This was probably the tip of the iceberg. Ben swallowed. "You said we wouldn't work. Yes, we will, Christina. We will."

She gave him another long look, then managed a nod.

He ran a hand over his mouth. "Do you love me?"

She started to cry again. "More than anything."

"And I love you too. I love you even more now than I did ten minutes ago. So trust me when I tell you—you just have to continue bein' honest with me. How do I know what you like and don't like if you don't tell me?"

She sniffed. "What if you don't like what I say?"

"Then we'll work it out. That's what love's all about."

That disbelieving look came back. He opened his mouth to say more—and sudden, cold understanding hit him. Christina had spent her whole childhood learning to hide her feelings just to survive. She'd never known honesty in a relationship. Never.

She hadn't a clue.

What if she didn't learn how to be honest? What if she couldn't trust him enough to overcome her past? She could ruin this for both of them. She really could.

He touched Christina on the arm, inwardly steeling himself for more. "Tell me somethin' else I do that you don't like."

She wiped away the last tear. "There is noth—"

"*Stop* it. That's not gonna work anymore."

She sighed, then sat in silence, her expression turning from soft to resolved, then back again. Finally her mouth opened. "I don't like the way your sisters wait on you."

What? "They don't wait on me."

"They do so. Anything you want, they run and fetch it for you."

Well, maybe they did. But he *liked* that. "So what's this got to do with us?"

"You'll expect me to do the same thing."

"No I won't."

"Yes you will. In fact you practically said so." Christina's head wagged. "'That's what I like—a woman who waits on me.'"

"I didn't mean that."

"You did, Ben. You *did*. You don't even realize how much you've been coddled as the baby of the family. *I'm* not going to do that. I waited on my parents all my life when they were too drunk to get up themselves—which was most of the time. I'm not doing that anymore."

Wait a minute, this was serious. "So ... you're tellin' me you're *never* gonna do *anything* for me?" Serving someone was a sign of love, wasn't it?

Christina made an exasperated noise. "I didn't say that."

"You just did."

"Well, I didn't mean never."

"Then what?"

"I mean, I don't want you to *expect* me to wait on you all the time. But I might choose to do it on my own."

"Oh."

They stared at each other.

Ben tapped his forefingers together. This honesty business was harder than he'd thought. "Okay. I won't expect you to wait on me."

Christina gave him a long look—*I'll believe it when I see it.* Then her face relaxed. "Okay."

Ben turned his head and looked at her out the corner of his eye. "Anything else?" He was almost afraid to ask.

"I think that's enough for now, don't you?"

His heart sank. "So there is more."

"No."

"But you said ..."

"I said that's enough."

"For now."

She shrugged. "I can't think of anything else."

Ben tipped his head back and regarded the ceiling. Why did she have to talk in circles? "Okay, Christina. If you do, you'll tell me. Right?" Except— what would he have to give up next?

"Yes."

"Promise?"

"I do."

No deceit in her expression.

Ben ran a hand through his hair. He felt plumb tuckered out. "Good."

He offered Christina a tentative smile, and she smiled back. Her smile grew wider, clearly from relief. "See?" He pushed a strand of hair behind her ear. "That wasn't so bad, was it?"

She shook her head and leaned forward to lie against his chest. Ben held her, feeling love bubble up. They'd just had their first ... whatever it was. And it had worked out just fine. Had to be all downhill from here.

Right?

79

CHAPTER 9

Ruth could hardly finish her apple pie. The worry over Ben and Christina swirled in her stomach as she lingered with the rest of the adults around the dining table. The three little ones had gone into their play room to watch TV.

Sarah took a satisfied drink of her coffee concoction. "Ben sure picked a fine time to 'talk.' Christina's latte's gettin' cold."

"Yeah, well, apparently they need it." Jess tossed her head. "You see the look on his face when Christina said her father was dead? I'll bet anything she hadn't told him that."

"How do you know?" Maddy pointed her fork at Jess.

"I was sittin' across the table from 'em. I saw it clear as day."

"I didn't see anything."

"Maddy, you don't see things if they're right in front of your face. I'm tellin' you, there's trouble in the Garden of Eden."

Ruth pushed her plate away. "Really, now, we shouldn't be talkin' about 'em. Whatever this is, they'll work it out."

She hoped. But she had to admit, she'd noticed Christina's nervous behavior too. Something about that girl just didn't sit right —

"Of course we have to talk about 'em," Jake said. "It's how the Dearing family does things. Gets in each others' business."

"Speak for yourself, Jake Samuels." Maddy gave him a look.

"Oh, come on, Miss Maddy. You don't think I heard later 'bout everything y'all said when Sarah and I were datin'? I think Jess even put down a bet we wouldn't make it."

"Speaking of." Sarah set down her mug. "Where's my money, sister?"

Jess sat back and folded her arms. "We did not bet."

"Did too." Sy regarded his daughter from under his eyebrows.

"Daddy! Whose side are you on?"

Sy's palms went up. "Neither. I'm on the side of the Lord."

"What?" Ruth laughed.

"He's quotin' the Bible. Sort of." Tamel grinned. "When the angel appeared to Joshua before battle."

"Know-it-all." Jess shook her head.

Ruth had to smile. "Knowing it all" was Jess's territory.

Tamel looked to Ruth. "Anyway, I agree with you. They'll work it out. Christina's a fine girl."

"How do you know?" Jess demanded.

"I got eyes. And gut instincts."

"Uh-huh."

Don arched his back. "Jake's right, it's not easy walkin' into this family. Y'all are tigher 'n' ticks on a dog leg, even if you don't act like it sometimes. I sure felt the once-over when I first got here."

Ruth dropped her hands on the table. "Don, I liked you the minute I saw you."

"What, you didn't like *me?*" Jake looked shocked.

"I didn't mean—"

"Mama Ruth," Tamel said, "*you* don't give anybody the once-over. You love everybody from the moment you see 'em."

"That's the truth." Sy gave a decisive nod.

"Aw, Tamel." Ruth shot him a silent thank-you. That was one of the nicest things anyone had ever said to her.

"I agree, best mama in the world." Jess smiled at Ruth, then smacked her palms together. "Now that's agreed on, let's get back to solvin' Ben's problems."

Maddy made a sound in her throat. "They'll solve 'em themselves, Jess."

"I'm not so sure. My guess is, Ben realizes durin' this reunion she's not the one for him."

Ruth shot her daughter a firm look. "Don't you dare go about tryin' to make that happen."

Jess pressed a hand to her chest—*me?*

"Yeah, Jessica." Sarah tapped a fingernail against her plate. "We already had this conversation."

Jess rolled her eyes. "I'm just sayin'. That girl has too much baggage."

"How do you know?" Don cleaned the last lick of pie off his plate.

"I just do."

Ruth and Sy exchanged a glance. "Listen now, all of you." Ruth's gaze went around the table. "Ben loves Christina. I've never seen him so happy. And we're goin' to do everything we can to help her into this family." Ruth leveled a look at Jess. "Right?"

"Sure." Jess waved a hand. "It's not that we're not tryin'. It's just that—I'm not sure she's gettin' it."

That comment spread a blanket of silence over the table. As she often did, Jess had hit the nail on the head. Ruth could only pray whatever the issues were, Ben and Christina would be able to overcome them.

By the time the couple returned, it was almost eight o'clock. Ruth and her three daughters were deep into dishes in the kitchen. Sy, Don, Jake, and Tamel sat in the adjoining den, talking all things male. Penny lay on Sy's lap. At the sound of the front door opening, Ruth's head jerked up. Seconds later the door closed.

Maddy eyed her. "Mom, stop worryin' now. You were the one who said everything would be fine."

Well. Those hadn't been her words exactly. "I know, I know."

Ben walked into the den, Christina right behind. The men stopped their conversation and greeted them both. Ruth gazed at her son's face. The expression she saw mixed relief, resolve, and more than a little anxiety.

"Hi, Ben." Ruth called. "Christina, we left your dessert on the table for you."

"Oh." She hesitated. "Thanks."

"Do you still want it? Or are you too full?"

Ben turned to watch her answer.

"I …" She glanced at Ben. "I'm kind of full now. Maybe later?"

84

"Sure."

Ben smiled and rubbed her shoulder.

"Your latte's still here too." Sarah pointed to the mug on the counter. "Little Brother rushed you off before you could even finish."

"Oh."

"Want me to nuke it for you?"

"Yes. I'd love to finish it." Christina shot Ruth a look, as if worried she'd offended her by accepting the latte and not the pie. Ruth gave her an animated shrug.

Just as Christina finished her latte, Lacey bounded out of the play room and grabbed her hand. "Come back and color with me."

Christina looked to Ben. He waved her on. "Lacey, don't wear her out, now."

The little girl giggled, as if that was an outrageous thought.

Ruth settled with the rest of the family in the den, talking and watching TV. Occasionally shrieks of laughter would filter from the play room. Twice Ben went to check on his fiancée. He came out the second time shaking his head. "They're in there colorin' up a storm."

An hour later Christina emerged, looking worn out, indeed. Ruth was beginning to feel tired herself. "Listen," she said to Christina, "if you're tired, go on to bed. We'll all be winding down here soon. And it's past the kids' bedtime anyhow."

"Thanks. I think I will." This time Christina didn't look to Ben for approval. He got up to walk her down the hall. Ruth and Sy exchanged knowing smiles.

Tamel said it was time for him to go. But not before egging Jess to take a ride with him the next day in his car.

Jess raised both hands. "And just why would I want to ride in that thing?"

"Don't you have to go into Jackson tomorrow?" Maddy flashed her sister a gotcha smile. She got a hard look in return.

"I can drive my own car, thank you very much."

"What do you have to go to Jackson for?" Tamel asked. Jackson was about thirty-five minutes away, up Highway 49.

"Actually I'm goin' to Ridgeland. I'm pickin' up the lobsters I ordered at Fresh Market, if you have to know." Ridgeland was north of Jackson.

"Not that she knows anything about cookin' lobster." Sarah wagged her head at Tamel.

"You just watch, smart aleck." Jess pointed at her. "I'm gonna make you a meal that'll blow your socks off."

"That bad, huh?" Maddy snickered.

They'd never had lobster at a family reunion before. Awful expensive meal. But Jess had been talking about it for weeks. The more her sisters doubted her, the more she aimed to prove them wrong. Said she had the perfect recipe to do just that.

Jess made a sound in her throat. "Why're y'all tryin' to get my goose today?"

"Every day's for gettin' your goose, little sister." Sarah shot her a sugary smile.

"Perfect." Tamel said the word with finality. "I'll take you to Ridgeland, Jess."

"No—"

"Thanks, Mama Ruth. Syton." Tamel hugged them both. "Wonderful dinner." On the way out he cocked a finger at Jess. "Call you in the mornin'."

Before she could reply, he turned toward the door. Jess put on her best peeved expression. Her older sisters grinned at each other.

It was way past the kids' bedtime. Their mothers got them down, then one by one the adults straggled off to their old bedrooms. Maddy's and Sarah's were downstairs, Jess's and Ben's on the second floor. As for Lady Penelope, she'd long since retired to her bed under the piano. Every once in a while she'd raised her head to cast a long-suffering look at the night owls—*can't you see you're bothering me while I'm trying to sleep?*

Ruth had lingered in the den, hoping to catch a word with Ben. When Sy rose to head upstairs, she sent him a silent message: *please stay.* He raised his eyebrows, then sat back down in his armchair. Finally only the two of them and Ben remained.

"Everything okay, Ben?" Ruth kept her voice low so it wouldn't filter down the hall.

He gave a slow nod. "She told me a bunch of things tonight I didn't know."

Ruth sat down on the couch beside him and waited him out. He might decide to talk, he might not. Sy clasped his hands and leaned forward. "What things?"

Ben sighed, then launched into a long narrative about Christina's childhood of terrible neglect and abuse. He spoke quietly but the words chilled Ruth to the bone. They also answered a lot of questions.

"Wow. That's just ... *awful.* The poor girl."

"I know."

"You're going to have to be very patient with her, Ben."

"I know that too."

Ruth processed that for a moment. Could he hang on to that patience? Being the child of alcoholics, suffering abuse all those years—these things stained the soul. They weren't overcome easily. Ruth wasn't sure Ben saw the depths of that reality.

Sy gestured with his hands. "She'll be fine. She's in our family now, and we'll all love her. Won't take her long to learn life can be very different from what she knew."

Ruth shot him a look.

"What?"

Men. Syton tended to look at everything through pure rationality. But things didn't always work that way. And Ben didn't need to hear that working through this kind of emotional baggage would be easy. He had to be prepared for it to be hard. He'd have to be ready.

"Ben, your dad's right. Of course we'll all nurture Christina and try to help her overcome the hurts. But this may take time. And her … issues may come up in unexpected ways in your relationship. You'll have to work through that. Some of the very things you might expect of your spouse—things ingrained because of your own childhood—may come in direct opposition to either what she expects, or what she's willin' to give. And don't forget—as much as I love you—it's not as if you're perfect yourself. You'll both have a lot to learn."

Ben stretched one side of his mouth. "What you said about expectations—that already came up tonight. Kind of an eye opener."

Sy sat back in his chair. "Main thing is, do you love her?"

"Yes. I *do* want this to work. I can't lose her. I know we only met a few months ago, but ... she's the one."

"Good. Then you know what to do. Same thing your mama and I have modeled for you kids all these years. You worry about Christina's comfort and happiness over your own. And she needs to worry about you over herself. You both put each other first, it doesn't leave room for selfishness and fights."

Sy was right—putting each other first had been the philosophy of their marriage from the beginning. That—and even more important—placing God at the center of the relationship.

"I know." Ben took a long breath. "But like you said, that takes two. And with all the stuff Christina has to work through, she may need to be more centered on herself awhile. That's what hit me when we were talkin' tonight."

Sy shrugged. "There's always times in a marriage when one person is more needy than the other. That's when the other one steps up. Gives more. The trick here is, Ben—the answer's not in takin'. The answer's in givin'. You may have to do an extra bit of that for a while. But if your wife really loves you and wants the marriage to work, she'll turn it around at some point."

Ben focused across the room, then nodded. "Yeah. I get that." His mouth curved down.

Ruth held back a smile. She could read his thoughts clear as day. The whirlwind "perfect" relationship had slipped, and he was realizing it would take some hard work to fix it. Young lovers always seemed to think it would be so easy ...

She patted her son's knee. "We'll be prayin' for both of you. Especially Christina. She's got a lot of bad hurts that we can only imagine. But God can heal those hurts. It's amazin' what His mercy can do."

Ben smiled at her. "Thanks." He sat a moment longer, then pushed to his feet. "I'm off to bed. See you in the mornin'."

Ruth and Sy got up to hug him. As Ben put his arms around Ruth, love and concern for him burst in her chest. She just wanted her son settled and happy.

"Good night, Ben."

In their own bedroom, Ruth and Sy exchanged a long, concerned look. One that spanned the years of their marriage, leaving no need for words.

Sy lifted a shoulder. "Like they say, 'Fallin' in love's easy; stayin' in love ain't.'"

Ruth stepped closer and hugged him hard. "But look what happens when you do."

CHAPTER 10

Saturday morning Jess woke up to kids' laughter downstairs and the voices of Maddie and Don in the bedroom below her. She opened one eye and checked her old digital clock. Seven-fifteen.

"Oh, sheesh." Jess flopped on her stomach and thumped a pillow over her head. She got up a lot earlier than this for her work days at the law firm of Dunham, Biggs and Tooley in Memphis. But this was supposed to be a mini-vacation.

For a couple minutes she daydreamed about taking a trip to Hawaii for once. Sleeping till noon, lazing the rest of the day away on the beach. Body surfing and stuffing herself at luaus.

Yeah, right. If she ever ditched a reunion for Hawaii, her family would strangle her.

With a sigh, Jess pulled herself out of bed and put on her running clothes. The good thing about getting up early was that she could do her four-mile run without seriously overheating. Half overheating she could handle.

Jess called good-mornings to the family members who were already up. No sign of Ben and Christina yet. Of course Mama was already in the kitchen, puttering.

Out on the road, Jess turned right toward town.

Jogging gave Jess uninterrupted time to think. Sometimes pray. And running through her hometown of Justus always seemed to ground her. This town was who she *was*. What she believed in. It could be easy to forget all that in the crazy days of reading briefs for businesses, advising on contracts, setting up corporations, or defending some client in court against a lawsuit. Not to mention trying to muscle her way up the ladder within the firm.

But wouldn't you know it—today she couldn't help thinking about Tamel Curd. That man just kept honing in on her life. No way was she driving to Ridgeland with him in that horrendous yellow hearse. What if someone she knew saw her in that thing?

Man, the day was hot already. She was already sweating bullets.

And just *what* was Tamel doing, living back in Justus? They'd been on the same track for years. Okay, they attended different colleges and law schools. Got incredibly busy jobs in different cities that left little time for socializing. Still, they were both attorneys with the same small-town background. They understood each other. Tamel had always been in the back of Jess's mind, even when they didn't talk on the phone for weeks. Their lives were entwined, going back to elementary school.

Now look what he'd done with himself. Ditched his career. Completely changed course. She'd have cried for him—if it didn't make her so furious.

He didn't deserve for her to be thinking about him

Jess tore her attention away from Tamel and focused on the familiar houses she passed. She ran through downtown, weaved through residential streets, then turned around and headed for home. By the time she walked in the door she was worn out. She headed straight for a cool shower. Goodness knows she had to smell worse than Pogey's feet.

The entire time she was getting ready, thoughts of Tamel Curd kept sneaking back into her brain.

Jess slipped into jean shorts and a hazel top that matched her eyes. Put on her makeup with care and fluffed up her hair. She checked herself in the mirror. Not bad, if she did say so herself.

In the kitchen Jess fixed herself an egg and toast and sat down at the table. The rest of the family was already milling about, Sarah and Maddy trying to feed kids and husbands, and Mama cleaning up behind. Dad was eating an omelet. Lady Penelope stayed out of the way, curled up on Dad's armchair. Christina and Ben stood close together in the kitchen, leaning against the counter. Both had mugs in their hands. Christina looked picture-perfect. Sarah and Maddy hadn't bothered with makeup yet.

Sarah poured Jess some coffee. Jess watched black oil dredge into her cup. "Oh, great, *you* made it."

Sarah gave her an over-sweet smile. "You're so welcome for your gratitude, sister dear."

Jess looked to Christina, who gave her an open smile. Hmm. The girl seemed a little more sure of herself this morning. "Sarah make you a latte again?"

"Yes. It's magnificent."

"*Magnificent?* Good grief, Christina, don't egg her on like that."

Christina looked at her mug, then busied herself taking a long sip.

Maddy put her hands on her hips. "You wake up on the wrong side of the shed, Jess?"

Ben and Sarah laughed. He leaned toward Christina. "Bed. She means wrong side of the bed."

Jess ignored them both.

"Or maybe she means Jess isn't the sharpest tool in the shed."

Jess glared at him.

"*I* know what's goin' on." Sarah sat down opposite Jess, acting like some Miss Priss know-it-all. "She's upset that Tamel hasn't called yet about drivin' her to Ridgeland."

Jess stuck her hands on her hips. "I can drive myself, thank you very much."

"Of course you could. But you won't. 'Cause deep down you want to be with him, and you know it."

"I do *not.*"

Mama gave a quick smile, then tried to hide it. Jess yanked at her toast and tore off a piece.

"Why're you so mad at Tamel?" Don turned his blue eyes on her. He worked in marketing for a large medical equipment company, and right now he looked at Jess as a sales problem to be solved.

"I am not mad at him." Jess set down her coffee cup none too gently. "I just want to be with my family and not have him comin' around. And would all of you quit *lookin'* at me?"

The phone rang.

Sarah was closest to the phone. "Gotta be him." She leaned back in her chair and checked the caller ID. "Yup."

Great. Jess was *not* taking this call in front of the entire ogling family.

Sarah snatched up the phone—oh, so happily. "Hi, Tamel. Yup, we're all eatin' breakfast. Here's Jess."

Maddy laughed. Don elbowed her, and she stuck a hand over her mouth.

Jess got up, took the receiver from Sarah and stalked out of the kitchen. "Hi, Tamel." She didn't stop until she was outside on the hot porch where no one could hear her.

"Hey, there, beautiful. Hope you're ready. I'm comin' over in fifteen minutes."

How had she never realized before how pushy Tamel could be? Man seemed to think he could run her life.

"I do not want to ride in that beastly car of yours."

"You sure are hard on Chiqui."

That was the other thing. He always acted so amused at everything she did. He'd just grin at her, all dimples and sparkling eyes. He'd teased her like that since they were in high school.

"I'm drivin' myself."

"Do you know how to pick the best lobsters?"

"I don't have to pick 'em. They've already been ordered."

"*I'm* the lobster guy."

"Oh, yeah, like you eat 'em all the time. What exactly is it you *can't* do, Tamel?"

95

A second passed. The silence pulsed in Jess's ears.

"Let me take you, Jess." Some of the lilt had gone out of Tamel's voice.

"Why?"

"Because I need someone to talk to."

Jess stared down the porch steps. What was this slip in the ever-optimistic Tamel?

Well, not surprising. No way could he be so cheery all the time. And he had to be lonely. After leaving his fast-paced job at a law firm to come back to tiny Justus? He had to be bored out of his mind.

"Okay."

Wait—she did say that?

"Great!" In an instant Tamel was back to his happy-go-lucky tone. "Pick you up soon."

The line went dead before she could protest.

Jess pulled the phone from her ear and narrowed her eyes at it. She'd been totally had.

CHAPTER 11

After breakfast Christina stood in her bathroom, checking her reflection with a critical eye. Maybe she looked a little better today. Her make-up and hair were half-working. At least that's how it seemed for the moment. If she could just keep up her pretense of having energy.

She'd hardly slept last night, after her and Ben's conversation. Fears pounded her, and she'd tossed and turned. Why had she said so much to him? How could she have opened up like that? Even if he did ask her to. Even if he got mad when she hesitated. In the end it would come back to haunt her. Ben might think he could love her for who she was. But really, most of what he'd seen was the competent side of her at work. The side that caught on quickly and did her job one hundred percent. Of course people at the company liked her for that. Of course her boss praised her.

This morning before breakfast Ben had taken her out to the front porch for a quiet conversation. "Thank you so much for talkin' to me last night, Christina. I loved hearin' about you. I love you all the more today." And he'd kissed her.

No doubt he meant it. But she'd only shown him one little edge of the iceberg of her past.

Pasting a pleasant expression on her face, Christina forced herself out of the bathroom to be with the family.

Only Mrs. Dearing, Maddy, and Sarah lingered at the kitchen table. Christina could hear the little girls chattering away in their play room. Jess had gone off to pick up the lobster with Tamel—even though she'd sworn up and down she wouldn't. Ben, Tommy, Don, and Mr. Dearing were getting ready for their golf game. The thought of being left behind in the Dearing household without Ben made Christina's heart flutter.

Penny sat on the couch, eyeing Christina. She looked so adorable.

"Hey there, cutie." Christina approached slowly, holding out her hand. Penny sniffed Christina's fingers, then put her chin on her paws. Christina eased onto the couch beside her and gave her some gentle pats.

"Christina, you want to join us?" Mrs. Dearing said. "We're just finishing our coffee."

Christina smiled at her. "I'm trying to keep this new friend I've made." If they only knew how much she'd wanted a dog as a child. She'd have done anything to cuddle one as darling as Penny.

Maddy nodded. "Looks like you're doin' pretty good."

Pogey walked into the family room, shoeless. Christina caught a whiff of smelly feet. Penny sneezed.

"She likes you." Pogey pointed at the Yorkie. "She doesn't like just anybody."

Christina's heart surged. "That's what Lacey said too."

Pogey made a face—*What does my sister know?* He stood looking at the dog, his sturdy legs spread, tongue working across the front of his teeth. Christina tried to think of something else to say.

"Pogey, is that your real name?"

"Naw, it's Peter."

"Oh." She waited for an explanation but none came. "How did people start calling you Pogey?"

"It's all Lacey's fault. When she was little she couldn't say Peter. She said Pogey. And it stuck."

"You don't sound too happy about that."

Pogey glanced at his grandmother and aunts. "Well, what're ya gonna do?"

Christina suppressed a smile.

He pointed at Penny. "Wanna hear her howl?"

"Now, Pogey, you'd better be careful." Sarah got up from the table, carrying dishes to the sink.

"Penny's already had a rough mornin'," Mrs. Dearing said. "I had to put her through her weekly tooth brushing. You know how she hates that. She always sticks out her tongue."

"I don't like brushin' my teeth, either." Pogey made another face.

"We know," his mother said.

Pogey came closer and touched Penny's nose. "She's really funny when she howls. She acts like

99

she's too uppity to do that, but if you play the piano and sing, she just can't help it."

Christina tilted her head. "My singing would make anybody howl. And I can't play the piano."

"I do. My mom makes me take stupid lessons."

"They are *not* stupid," Sarah said.

Pogey marched to the piano and sat down on the bench. "She likes this song. Penny, I mean." He started to play a simple rendition of "Somewhere Over the Rainbow."

Penny's head came up. Her ears pricked forward as she watched Pogey's back.

"But ya gotta sing." Pogey started the song over, singing along. Out came a surprisingly clear voice. "Somme wherrre oover the raiiinbow, way up hiiiigh..."

Christina raised her eyebrows. "That's really nice, Pogey."

The ten-year-old glanced over his shoulder. "C'mon, Penny. Sing with me." "Theeere's a land that I've heard of once in a lullllaaaabyyyy."

Penny made a noise in her throat and put her head back down as if she wanted none of it. She closed her eyes, but they popped back open. She lifted her head once more.

"Somme wherrre oover the raiiinbow, skies arre bluuuue. Aand the dreeeams that you dare to dream really doo comme truuuue."

Christina glanced at the women in the kitchen. Maddy brought a finger to her lips and whispered, "Whatever you do, don't laugh."

"Someday I'll wish upon a star and wake up where the clouds are far behiiiiind meee."

Lady Penelope popped up on her feet like a puppet. She lingered on the couch for a second, then

100

jumped down. Head held high, she trotted regally to the piano and sat at the side of the bench. Her dark brown eyes watched Pogey.

"Where troubles melt like lemon drops, away above the chimney tops, that's wherrre youuuu'll fiiiiind meeeee."

Penny's nose started to rise in the air. She pushed it back down.

"C'mon, Penny. Ya know you can't help it. Somme wherrre oover the raiiinbow, bluuue birrrds flyyyy."

The Yorkie made a funny little sound in her throat. Her head tipped back, back, until her brown nose reached into the air like those of her wolf ancestors. Christina felt a giggle kick up inside her. She pressed fingers over her lips.

"Birrrds fly oover the raiiinbow."

Lady Penelope's mouth opened, her jaw stretching forward.

"Why, then, oh why can't Iiii."

A gritty little rumble began low in Penny's throat, then spilled out her open snout. "Aaaaoooooooo ..." It rose in pitch until she almost matched Pogey's note.

Pogey's shoulders shook in a quiet laugh, but he kept singing. "If happy little bluebirds fly ..."

The howl got louder. "Ooooooooooooooo ..."

"Beyond the rainbow ..."

"Oooooooooooooo ..."

"Whyyy, ohhhh, whyyyy ..."

"Oooooooooooooo"—a doggie gasp— "aauuooooooooooo ..."

Laughter bounced around inside Christina. She glanced at Mrs. Dearing, Sarah, and Maddy. All three had hands pressed to their mouths.

"Caaaan't ..."

"Ooooooooo …"

"Iiiiiii?"

Penny's last note split in two, a lower rumble and a high mini-coyote howl.

A chortle exploded from Christina. She tried to gulp it back, but it was too late. Penny's nose jerked down. Her head snapped toward Christina. The Yorkie's back straightened, as if she realized how far she'd fallen in her moment of weakness. Her little brown eyes narrowed, and her ears went back. She looked so downright doggie *mad*. Christina clutched her sides, trying not to laugh more, but giggles spilled out of her.

"Uh-oh." Pogey looked from her to Lady Penelope.

Stiffly the dog rose to her feet. She faced Christina in a long moment of scathing, royal anger, then huffed around in a half-circle and pointed herself in the opposite direction. With utmost dignity she stalked to the far empty corner until her nose practically touched the wall. Then she sat down, back hunched. Her ears flattened. Everything about her body language declared *I'd rather stick my nose in this empty corner than look at the likes of despicable you.*

Laughter gurgled from someone at the kitchen table. Penny's ears twitched.

Pogey turned toward Christina. "She's givin' you The Treatment 'cause you laughed."

"I'm s-sorry." But she couldn't stop giggling. Oh, her stomach hurt.

Lady Penelope gave her little head a slow turn until she glared lasers at Christina over her shoulder. Then she pointed her nose back into the corner.

Christina's eyes started to water. She wiped at them. "How long will she stay like that?"

Pogey shrugged. "Long as it takes. You ain't gonna be pettin' her now."

Oh, no. The laughter in Christina died away. She'd turned Penny against her for good? What had she done? "Should I go over and try to make it up to her?"

"Definitely not." Sarah spoke up from the sink. "She'll walk away all the madder. Just let her be, she'll get over it."

From the looks of Penny, that wouldn't be anytime soon.

"I'm sorry." Christina's throat went thick. "I didn't mean to."

Mrs. Dearing waved a hand. "We've all done the same thing. Penny's just too funny. You should've seen the first time she howled. Syton and I nearly ended up on the floor. Lady P. didn't speak to us for two days."

Two days? She and Ben would be gone by then. Christina swallowed hard. Not a good way to start the morning. Now she faced four to five hours without Ben while he played golf. And she wouldn't be passing the time by cuddling Penny.

Pogey slid off the piano bench. He glanced at Christina and gave her a wrinkled-nose grin. "Don't worry 'bout it."

Footsteps pounded down the front stairs. "All right!" Ben's voice. "Let's get this show on the road." He strode into the family room and spotted Penny in the corner. "Uh-oh. Somebody laugh at her?"

Christina looked at her lap. She felt rather than heard a silent exchange between Ben and his mother. Ben walked over and ran his hand across the top of Christina's head. "Hey, don't look so downhearted.

103

She'll forgive you." Tease crept into his voice. "Someday."

The word *hurt*. Christina felt it ping around inside her—then looked up and managed a smile.

"There ya go." Ben winked.

Penny's nose stayed in the corner.

Mr. Dearing, Jake, and Don soon appeared, all dressed and sun-screened for golf. A whirlwind of activity followed as everyone said goodbye. Ben kissed Christina. "Be back soon—in victory." He grinned. "You keep out of trouble, you hear?" He swiped a finger down the top of her nose.

He was teasing again, but he shouldn't be. If there was another big no-no for her to do, she'd probably manage it.

Heavy-hearted, Christina stepped out on the porch to wave goodbye as Mr. Dearing backed out the driveway. The air was so hot and muggy. The men would fry out on the golf course. What could they possibly see in that game?

Ben waved back and blew her a kiss.

Christina watched the car disappear down the road, then forced herself back inside. Alone.

CHAPTER 12

So here sat Jess, riding in the front passenger seat of Tamel's banana hearse. Only thing worse would be riding in back where the corpses used to lie. Jess couldn't help but be a little extra frosty toward Tamel for twisting her arm to say yes to this venture. Her sisters hadn't helped things any. When they heard she was letting Tamel take her to Ridgeland, they practically crowed their way out of the kitchen.

"Awww, I *knew* you'd go!" Maddy clapped her hands together.

Goody for her.

"Oh, c'mon, Jess, don't look so put out. You can't hide your head in the surf forever."

Jess gave her sister a *you-idiot* look. "Surf, Maddy?"

Sarah laughed. "Try sand."

"Don't get me off the subject." Maddy folded her arms. "You know good and well Tamel's in love with you, and you at least like him back — a lot. You just won't admit it."

"Are you out of your mind? What would I want with some guy who runs a funeral parlor in Justus, Mississippi?"

"Careful now." Mom stepped in from the east wing hallway. "Better watch the way you talk about your hometown."

"It's not the hometown, it's the man —"

That's when the doorbell had rung. Tamel, right on time.

Now Tamel sat in his tacky-hearse driver's seat, one tanned hand on the wheel. His bright blue knit shirt offset the chocolate brown of his eyes. For some reason those eyes weren't quite as sparkly today. Jess felt some of her frostiness melt. It was a lot easier to dig at him when he was in his smiley know-it-all mood. Which was most of the time.

"Tamel, what's a hearse doin' with two coffee cup holders?" She pointed to the console.

"I had 'em put in."

"What in the world for?"

He halted at a stop sign and turned to look at her. "You want some coffee?"

"As a matter of fact, I do. Dear sister Sarah made her witch's brew this morning, which I couldn't drink." Jess effected a shudder.

"That's why I put in the holders. Sometimes people want to drink somethin'."

"Well, duh."

"You asked."

Wasn't he a smart aleck this morning? As if he could afford to be, driving a monstrous vehicle like this. When they reached the bigger towns, she'd have to duck down in the seat. "Can we go through Mocha Ritaville?"

"Yeah. Unless you want to wait till we get near the seafood store."

No way, she wasn't stopping at a coffee place outside Justus in this car. "Nope. Besides, I wanna see you make Rita's day."

"Oh, boy."

Rita Betts was like no one else. But then, that could describe half the people in Justus. Pushing sixty, Rita acted like some hippie teenager caught in a time warp. She was the only white woman Jess knew with dreadlocks. Lots of them, down past her shoulders. Rita's eyes were hazel green, and she caked on purple eye shadow. Her arms jangled under heavy bracelets. Years of sporting dangly earrings had pulled down the holes in her ears.

In the downtown block Tamel turned right onto Grant Street and pulled up to the free-standing express coffee hut. The car was twice as long as the little building. He rolled down the window as Rita Baxter peered out from her perch inside. Jess could hear Mocha Ritaville's ever present Jimmy Buffet music playing.

"Well, if it ain't the handsome Tamel Curd." Rita's deep, throaty voice betrayed her years of smoking. "Who you got with ya there?" Rita bent down until she met eyes with Jess. "Oh, my, Jessica Dearing." Rita looked at them askance, as if she knew exactly what was up with the two of them. Give it an hour, and she'd have the news they were together all over town. Probably have them getting married next week.

"How's the lawyer business, Jess?"

Tamel's smile fell a little, then jumped back onto his face.

"It's fine. Good to see you, Rita."

Today Rita's earrings were big shiny red bead-like affairs. Interesting match to her orange tee shirt.

"Tamel, you handsome devil, when're you gonna marry me?"

Rita's line for years now.

He grinned. "I'm workin' on it, Rita. I just don't know how I'd keep you in the luxury to which you've grown accustomed." He waved his hand at the coffee express.

"Honey, livin' in a *shack* with you would be luxury." She flashed a wide, flirtatious smile, showing yellowed teeth.

Yikes and boy howdy, as Granddad Pete used to say.

"You must have a free day today, Mr. Curd." Rita winked at Tamel. "I ain't heard a nobody dyin' lately."

Tamel flicked his hand. "Nope, nobody died, I'm afraid."

Rita threw back her hand and hooted. "What a life! Waitin' fer people to kick the bucket!"

Tamel kept on smiling, but Jess could tell the comment pricked.

Rita pounded her wooden window sill to calm herself down. "Y'all hear 'bout Leslie Willis?"

They both shook their heads.

"Well, you know she turned sixty last Sunday. Still claims she's thirty-nine. Not that anybody believes that bag a wrinkles, bless her heart. Anyway, she done found herself a man in Florence a good twenty years younger 'n' her. Got him up livin' in her house, fetchin' her mail and food at the grocery."

"Oh." Tamel raised his chin. He wasn't much for Justus gossip.

"That ain't the kicker." Rita flicked an earring around in a dramatic pause. "Young Romeo's her son's best friend."

"Which son—Tony?"

Tony Willis ran the one gas station in town. "The one and only. So now he's all bent outta shape, not talkin' to his mama 'cause he says she's shamed him. They had a fight last night, and he got so mad he stomped down her porch stairs and fell and broke a leg. So now he cain't work at the station, and that's why it's closed."

"The Justus station's *closed*?" Tamel stuck his chin forward.

"Yup, fer now. Hope you ain't needin' any gas."

Tamel and Jess exchanged a look. That station had been in business as long as they could remember.

"What about his help, Charlie and Tom?" Tamel asked. "Can't one of them take over for a while?"

Rita gave her head a slow shake, mouthing *Noooo*. "Way I heard it, Leslie's so mad at her son she called both them boys and said she'd sic her new man on 'em if either one set foot in the station—Tony deserves to lose the business. And her new man weighs near three hundred pounds."

Jess choked back a laugh. Tamel raised a hand— *what can you say?*

Rita shifted on her feet, leaning on one fat arm. She looked mighty pleased about telling Jess and Tamel this juicy piece of news.

Her expression changed to all business. "So." She shifted again, hitting the drive-up window ledge with a palm. "What can I getcha?"

109

Tamel ordered a double latte, and Jess, black coffee. Tamel insisted on paying. Rita proposed to him twice more before he could close his window and drive away.

"Man, she is somethin'." Jess cradled her cup.

"Yeah."

"Poor Tony."

"And Charlie and Tom. I hope we get our gas station back."

"The town'll be up in arms if you don't. They'll run Leslie's new boyfriend back to Florence."

Tamel grunted.

Silence fell over the car. Jess studied Tamel. He looked bothered. If he knew she was watching him, he didn't let on.

What was this, a new tactic to draw her out? He was usually the talker.

They passed the outskirts of Justus and headed north on Highway 49.

"So what's goin' on, Tamel? You said you needed to talk to someone."

"Actually no. I needed to talk to *you*."

Oh. Jess worked her mouth. "So talk."

Tamel threw her an exasperated look. "Why are you always like that these days?"

"Like what?"

"You know very well what I'm talkin' about."

"No, I don't."

"I—" He lifted a hand and let it drop. "Fine."

Jess took her time placing her coffee in the empty console holder.

"When did we last see each other, Jess?"

"Easter." He knew that.

"And before that?"

"Christmas."

110

"Either time, did you act happy to see me? Or more like you were just continuously ticked off?"

"I ... I don't know." Why was he being so direct all of a sudden?

"Well, I do. And it's the latter."

Jess bit the inside of her lip.

"And when did we see each other before that?"

She didn't have to think very hard. "Last August. Our last family reunion. You came home for the weekend." Tamel had still been working at the law firm in Biloxi, about two hours and forty minutes from Justus.

"Remember what we did?"

Jessica's heart pricked. She looked out the window. "Yes."

"We hung out together as much as we could without takin' you away from your family. We took a drive. Had a late-night snack Saturday night in Jackson."

"Mm-hm." She felt a lump in her throat. It had been a great weekend. But that was before. When he was still an attorney, doing what he was meant to do. Now look at how he earned his living—if you could call it that.

She didn't even know him anymore.

Tamel rubbed his forehead. "These last ten months since I've been back in Justus have been some of the longest of my life. I've really looked forward to your comin' home. But Christmas, Easter, and now—all you do is act cold toward me." Hurt coated his voice. "I've kept upbeat around you, kept smilin', but it's gettin' pretty old, Jess."

Jess gazed at her lap, cut to the core. How could she have known? He always acted so sure of himself, as if what she did made no difference. But a voice

111

deep inside her told her to stop rationalizing. She had to have known she was hurting him. Tamel wasn't a cold person, far from it.

"I'm sorry." Her words were barely a whisper.

Tamel took a deep breath. "What I want to know is — why?"

Shame trickled through Jess, trailing defensiveness. He had to know why. He was just making her say it. And the reason made her feel about two feet tall.

"I'm listenin'. And I'm not gonna let this drop."

"Fine then, Tamel Curd." She folded her arms. "Because you walked away from a great career, that's why."

"Ah. You mean because I came back to help my father, who happens to be dyin'?"

He'd die anyway, wouldn't he?

The minute she thought the words, Jess felt appalled at herself. But it was true, wasn't it? Henry Curd had never been much of a father to Tamel. Now he wanted to ruin his son's life by forcing him to take over the funeral parlor. And Tamel was just going along with it.

"You could have helped him and kept your job. Come to visit more often. Get him to sell his business. He should be retirin' anyway."

"That's not what he wanted."

"What did *you* want, Tamel? Doesn't that count?"

Tamel's eyes remained locked on the road, his jaw set. When he spoke again, his voice was quiet. "What I wanted was to forge as much of a relationship with my father as I could during his remainin' days. I never had a dad like yours, Jess. And I lost my mama long ago. You don't know what it's like to want for more in your family."

112

Jess couldn't find a response.

"My father's likely to die within a year."

She looked at Tamel, eyebrows raised. "I didn't know he was that bad."

"How could you? You've never come 'round to see."

Jess bit her lip and turned away.

Tamel said no more.

Jess unfolded her arms. Clasped her hands. "So ... what will you do then?"

"He wants me to stay in Justus. Keep runnin' the business."

"I know." The thought infuriated her. Selfish old man. Didn't care about his son at all. "So is that what you're goin' to do?"

"I suppose if I did, you'd never speak to me again."

"I never said that."

"No. You *act* it."

He made her sound so ... petty. She wanted to smack him. "For your information, we'd still be friends."

"Oh, good. Like we are now. The up-and-comin' Memphis attorney lookin' down her nose at her childhood friend. 'Tsk, tsk, see what he's made of his life. And he had so much potential.'"

"I've *never* talked to you like that."

"You don't have to, Jess!" He tossed her a glare. "It's written all over you."

"I—"

"You've always been pretty self-absorbed. I figured as you got older you'd grow out of it."

"How dare—"

"But your self confidence, the way you take life by the horns—that's what I've always admired about

113

you. You've been that way since grade school. And in high school you were the shinin' light over everyone. No one could touch you, Jess. No other girl came *close* to you."

What was this? One minute he was cutting her down ...

She waited for him to say more, but Tamel fell silent. She could feel frustration coming off him. It was in the way he gripped the steering wheel, watched the road like it was going to roll up and blow away.

Jess pushed tease into her tone. "So I'm not a shinin' light anymore?"

"More like shallow waters."

"Oh. Well, aren't you Mr. Deep Ocean."

No response.

"And what makes me so 'shallow' all of a sudden?"

He threw her another hard glance, as if she knew very well.

"Okay, Tamel. Have it your way. I'm shallow because I think you shouldn't have given up your career. Forgive me for being sorry to see all your hard work go for nothin'."

"I'm helpin' my dad."

"Yeah. I get it."

"Wouldn't you help yours?"

Her dad would never ask her to change her career and goals. He wouldn't suck the life out of her like that.

"*Wouldn't* you?"

Oh, for— "You never answered *my* question. What are you gonna do after your dad is gone?"

"Why does it matter to you?"

"It matters a lot! I don't want to see you throw your life away, just for the wishes of a parent who's not even around anymore!"

"Because I wouldn't be equal to you, right? I'd just be some small-town hick."

"Wait a minute, I love Justus. I grew up here too."

"This isn't about the town. It's about how you view people who grow up here and choose to stay. Maybe some people don't like city life. Maybe they want to be in an easier-paced atmosphere."

"Good for them. We're talkin' 'bout *you*."

Tamel drummed his fingers on the steering wheel. "I'd be the same person, Jess."

"Is that a yes? You're gonna *stay*?"

"I'd *be* the same person."

But he wouldn't, that was just it. He already wasn't. How can you be the same when you give up your goals and settle for so much less?

"Tamel, *don't*. You can sell your dad's business then. There'll be no point in your stayin'. You can come to Memphis. I'll help you get a job in a firm somewhere." Hadn't they both known someday they'd be near each other? That one day—

"I get it, Jess. Then I'd be back up to your level, so you'd like me again."

She narrowed her eyes at him, then twisted away to glare out the windshield.

Tamel said no more.

They reached Ridgeville. Tamel stopped at a red light and stared straight ahead.

Tears pricked Jess's eyes. She blinked them back. No way on this earth would she let Tamel Curd think he'd made her cry. No way would she let him

115

think she cared one whit about him. And he had no right to judge her. *She* hadn't gone off course, *he* had.

Tamel had ticked her off so bad, she'd almost forgotten the monstrosity she was riding in. When other drivers stared, she ignored them.

After two more simmering miles, they reached Fresh Market. Jess opened her door to get out, but Tamel didn't move. "Aren't you comin' inside?" The guy who knew so much about lobsters?

"No."

"Fine then." Jess slammed the ugly yellow door and stalked away. Why in the world hadn't she driven herself here?

Inside the store it took some doing to shove her anger aside long enough to visit the seafood department and pick up the lobsters. She'd ordered nine of them, one for each adult—*not* including Tamel. The kids would be eating hamburgers.

And so what if they were expensive? She'd known this would cost a lot. She was a lawyer with a good job—unlike someone she knew. Jess Dearing could afford it.

Ten minutes later she exited the store, victorious in lobsters and a whole lot poorer. She carried three paper bags full of moving live creatures, each of them with wide colored rubber bands over their pinchers. She tossed the bags in the back of the car, then hefted herself up front. Ol' Camel wouldn't even look at her.

Jerk.

They drove home in silence, vibrations roiling in the car. From the back came eerie scraping sounds of claws against paper. Panicked lobsters, not quite knowing what had hit 'em.

Jess felt the same way.

Twice during the drive fresh tears scratched at her eyes. Each time she blinked them back. When they reached the house, she grabbed her purse and got out. Fetched her haul from the back. Before closing the rear door she made one last effort. "You comin' to supper?" It was the polite thing to say, not that he deserved it. She'd share her lobster.

"Nope."

Not even a "thank you" for the offer.

"Good for you. Thanks for the ride." She slammed the door.

He drove off without looking back. She couldn't help but stand there and watch him go.

Good riddance out of my life, Tamel Curd.

CHAPTER 13

Christina found the house so quiet with Jess and the men gone. She would have loved to play with Lady Penelope, but the stubborn Yorkie still had her nose stuck in the corner.

"How long is she going to stay like that?" Christina asked Sarah, who lingered in the kitchen, Lacey at her side.

Sarah shrugged. "Long as she figures it takes to punish you."

Christina already felt punished.

Sarah must have seen her fallen expression. "Don't worry, the dog'll get over it." She turned toward Penny. "Hear that, Lady P? You're a *dog*."

Maybe. But she clearly thought she'd descended from royalty.

Mrs. Dearing came into the kitchen and bustled about, making a list of things to get at the store.

"Okay, I'm ready, Sarah, let's go." She turned to Christina. "Want to come with us, hon?"

"No, stay and play!" Lacey stood up on her toes. "We can color."

Which should she do? Either way, someone wouldn't be happy with her.

"Oh, have mercy, I have a headache." Maddy appeared in the family room, headed for the kitchen. She opened a cabinet and pulled out a bottle of pain reliever.

"Oh, dear, I'm sorry." Mrs. Dearing frowned. "Somethin' we can get you at the store?"

"No, these'll do." Maddy stuck two pills in her mouth and gulped them down with water.

"Maybe I should stay," Christina said. "I'll watch the kids, and Maddy can rest."

"Oh, goody, I'm gonna go pick some colorin' books!" Lacey skipped down the west wing hall, then veered into the play room. Christina could hear one of Pogey's video games already running.

"That sure is nice of you, Christina." Mrs. Dearing picked up her purse. "You sure you'll be all right?"

No. "Sure."

"Okay. Thank you." She checked the clock. "Jess has been gone about forty-five minutes. If they go to the seafood store and come straight home, she'll be back in a half hour or so." She turned to Maddy. "You lie down now, hear? Get rid of that headache before everybody gets home."

"Don't worry, I'm goin' back to bed."

Mrs. Dearing and Sarah disappeared down the hall toward the garage.

Maddy put the bottle on the shelf. "You're a darlin', Christina."

"No problem. Do you get headaches very often?"

In childhood Christina had a lot of stomach aches. They'd gone away when she fled her parents' house.

"Not really. But they're doozies when I do. Best thing is to take some aspirin and lie down." She raised her voice toward the play room. "Lacey, y'all keep it quiet in there now."

"Yes, ma'am."

"Alex, don't you fight with your cousin."

"Yes, Mama," Alex's little voice squeaked.

Maddy ambled off down the east wing hallway.

For a moment Christina stood in the empty family room, watching Penny. The Yorkie must have sensed most everyone had gone. She peeked over her shoulder, spotted Christina, and gave her a hard look.

"Hi, Penny. Will you please forgive me?" Christina took a step forward.

Penny's ears went back. She turned around and faced the corner.

Great. Christina couldn't even get the dog to like her. And the day had just begun.

"Christina, come on!" Lacey's voice filtered from the play room.

"Coming."

Soon she was ensconced at the large play table, coloring with the girls. Books and crayons littered the table, as well as child scissors, paper, pens, and pencils. Mrs. Dearing sure kept the place well stocked. Pogey sat on the floor cross-legged, eyes locked on his TV video game. Lacey and Alex played quietly awhile, then started squabbling about who would color a fairy princess on a certain page. Their argument got louder and louder. Christina started to sweat.

"Shh, you have to be quiet. You don't want to wake up your mom, Alex."

"But I want the picture!" She pushed out her lips in an exaggerated pout.

This little girl was spoiled. If Christina ever had kids, she'd love them like crazy, but she'd wouldn't stand for this. "Well, you can't have it if you're going to fight about it."

"You can't give it to Lacey!"

"Why can't she?" Lacey looked just fine with the idea.

Christina reached for the picture. "I'll take it and not give it to either of you."

"*You're* not my mama." Alex narrowed her eyes.

Oh, please. Pogey kept on playing his game, no help at all.

Christina took a deep breath and manufactured a smile. "No, I'm not. But I'd like to play without fighting, and your mom needs to rest."

"We *are* playing, and *I* want the picture." Alex pushed up from the table, her face dark. "I'm gonna go tell." She stomped toward the door.

"No, wait!" Christina swallowed. "How about if we get something to eat?"

Alex turned back and eyed her with suspicion. "Like what?"

Christina thought a minute. "I'll bet there's some apple pie left."

Lacey screwed up her face. "Apple pie after breakfast? My mama'd be mad."

Great. Which mother to have angry at her, Maddy or Sarah?

Maddy would be in the worst mood, given her headache. Besides, Christina felt sorry for her. "Well, maybe we'll do it and not tell."

Lacey slid a look at her brother. "Pogey'll tell."

"Pogey doesn't even hear us." The boy was totally lost in cyber land.

Lacey and Alex exchanged looks. Alex unfolded her arms. "I want some pie."

"Okay, let's go." Christina got up before they could change their minds. They followed. She led the girls into the kitchen, praying she'd find some apple pie. She was in luck—half of a pie still sat in the refrigerator.

"I want ice cream with mine," Alex whined

Of course she did. Christina gritted her teeth and opened the freezer door.

Quickly she fixed the plates and set them before the girls. Since Alex was having ice cream, of course Lacey had to eat some too. They both happily dug in, Lacey swinging her feet. From the look on her face, she was pleased as punch to be getting away with something her mama would never let her do.

This couldn't be setting a good precedent. But Christina would have to worry about that later.

The girls continued to eat, no fighting. Maybe, Christina thought, she just might get away with this before Jess got home. If the girls would just finish. They were taking forever. Alex took a bite about every other minute.

The front door opened. Christina tensed.

Lacey's head jerked up. Her mouth was full of pie. "Izza my ma?"

No way, Sarah couldn't be back that soon. Besides, she'd be coming in from the garage. "I'll check." Christina bounced up.

On her way through the family room she vaguely noticed Lady Penelope sleeping in her doggie bed. Apparently Christina's punishment was over.

She rounded the corner. Jess stood in the front hallway, purse over her shoulder. Carrying three paper bags, which were strangely moving. Anger tightened her lips. In fact every muscle in her body looked hard as granite.

Wonderful.

She held up the bags almost in defiance. "Lobsters."

"Oh."

"And Tamel is *not* comin' to dinner, if you'd like to know."

Oh. Christina nodded awkwardly.

Jess eyed her. "So what's wrong with *you*?"

"I ... nothing."

"Uh-huh." She stomped past Christina, lugging the bags. "Everybody's crazy today."

Christina trotted behind, heart tripping. As they entered the family room, Christina glanced at the girls. They sat at the table, no plates, no pie, gazes fixed on their aunt. Guilt all over their faces.

Jess halted. "What's goin' on with you two?"

Lacey raised innocent eyebrows. "Nothin'."

"Why're you just sittin' there?"

Alex shrugged.

Jess turned to face Christina. "What's goin' on? Where's their mamas?"

Christina could hardly find her voice. "Sarah and Mrs. Dearing are at the store. And Maddy's in bed with a bad headache. I was tryin' to keep the girls quiet ..."

124

"Apparently you succeeded. I've never seen 'em just sit at a table before. What'd you do, feed 'em Prozac?"

Alex jerked. Her hands flew beneath the table, as if grabbing for something. A clatter sounded on the kitchen tile floor. Alex's face registered shock, then dissolved in tears.

"Oh!" She let out a wail.

Jess tipped back her head, as if accusing the heavens for her rotten day. "Alex, *what*?"

Christina ran to Alex's side and pulled back her chair. Her half eaten slice of pie and ice cream glopped on the floor, the plate shattered. A fork lay underneath the mess.

"*Look* at my *clothes!*" Alex's voice rose as she pointed. Half of the food smeared across her bright yellow shorts and the bottom of her blue shirt. She cried louder.

"Shh!" Panic gripped Christina. She placed her palms on Alex's cheeks. "Don't worry, I'll clean it up."

"I'm all *dürrrr-teee!*"

"*Please* be quiet."

"Waaaahh!"

"Good grief, Alex, can it!" Jess marched into the kitchen and dropped her bags in the sink.

Alex shook off Christina's hands and cried louder.

Surely Maddy could hear. Christina cast a pleading look to Jess. "I promised Maddy we wouldn't wake her up."

Jess strode over to Alex and pulled her off the chair. "You want me to make you sit in the garage all by yourself? 'Cause I'm in no mood to put up with you."

125

Alex shook her head hard.

"Then shut up."

The little girl gulped and clamped her mouth closed, breathing hard.

"That's better." Jess straightened and focused on Lacey. "You eatin' pie too?"

Lacey hesitated, then nodded.

"Well, get it off your lap before you lose it."

The near empty plate appeared on the table, along with a fork.

Jess thrust a hand on her hip. "What're you doin' eatin' pie in the mornin'?"

Alex swiped at her face and sniffed. Any minute she'd start wailing again. She focused on her lap and pointed to Christina.

Oh, God, help.

Jess swung to Christina. "This what you do in Texas?"

"I just ... I needed to keep 'em quiet, and they were fightin'..."

Jess raised a mocking hand—*Of course, what else could you do?* "Whatever. Clean 'em up, would you? I gotta go stick these lobsters in the garage sink." She towered over Alex. "And don't you *dare* start cryin' again. You wake up your mom with a headache, she's liable to whack you one."

Christina's eyes widened. Maddy wouldn't do that. Would she?

Jess yanked up the bags and barged down the hall toward the garage.

Christina's legs felt shaky. "Okay, Alex." She tried to keep her voice calm. "Let's get you cleaned up."

Alex shot her an accusing stare. "I have to put on different clothes."

126

"That's fine —"

"How'm I gonna do that without wakin' up my mama?"

Oh. Right. Her stuff was in Maddy's room. "Lacey, can she borrow some of your clothes for a while?"

"She's smaller 'n' me."

"I don't *want* her shorts, I want *mine*." Alex's pout roared back.

Christina heaved a sigh. *Why* hadn't she gone to the store? "Okay, tell you what. I'll wash and dry your shorts and top right now. You should be able to put them back on soon."

But not before Sarah and Mrs. Dearing came back from the store. Not good. This was going to get worse.

"What'm I supposed to do while you're washin' 'em?"

"Do you have anything in another room?"

"How 'bout you wear my nightgown?" Lacey sounded like the older, wiser cousin. "You like it."

Alex frowned at the table. "Okay."

Relief surged through Christina. She hugged Lacey. "Thanks so much, big girl."

Lacey looked proud of herself. "I'll go get it." She scampered on mice feet toward the east wing.

Christina began to clean up the mess on the floor. She'd have to throw the broken dish away. Mrs. Dearing would surely notice a plate missing.

Jess appeared, carrying empty paper bags. She still looked sour. "Don't worry about the plate." She waved a hand. "Happens every reunion. I'm goin' up to my room."

127

Lacey came back, toting a bright pink nightgown. Alex stripped off her offending clothes and slid into it.

"Okay." Christina wiped the last of the food off the tile. "Can you girls go back to coloring now and not fight? Don't use the fairy princess page. Both of you do something else."

"Oh, she can have it." Lacey's voice bulged with tolerance. She headed down the hall, still in her helpful role of older cousin. Alex followed.

"Where's the washer and dryer?" Christina called after them. She had to do this in a hurry.

Lacey pointed toward the garage. "Down there."

Christina scurried down the hallway. The garage sat empty, both cars gone. Neatly packed boxes lined built-in shelves on the far side. Toward the back was a door. Christina hurried through it and found a good sized laundry room. Dryer, washer, and a huge deep sink beyond that at the far end. Ironing board and iron. A long line of cabinets with plenty counter space for folding.

Fast as she could, she dumped the clothes in the washer, followed by soap from a nearby box of detergent. Flipped the machine to its smallest load, warm water, and turned it on. Water swished into the machine.

She staggered back through the garage. In the kitchen she gulped a glass of water.

Now ... *breathe.*

She leaned against the counter, dreading the moment when the two women came home. And Maddy got up. They'd all be so mad at her. Jess was already ticked. Not to mention Penny.

She was totally failing with everybody.

128

Shoulders drooping, Christina walked into the family room and slumped onto the couch. Would this reunion ever be over? She still had today and all of tomorrow.

She turned her head to look at Penny, still in her bed. The Yorkie's eyes locked on hers, then closed dismissively—*Don't even think about coming over here.*

Fine. Be that way.

Christina lay her head back against the couch cushion and started to cry.

CHAPTER 14

Man, it was hotter 'n' blazes on the golf course. They'd teed off at nine twenty-five and were only on the third hole. Ben was already sweating like a pig. He wore a cap low over his eyes to block out the sun's glare. Jake, Don, and Dad wore hats, too. They all had water bottles. Ben's was half empty.

It was Ben's turn to play—last of the foursome. The other three men weren't doing so great. At least at this short hole they'd all gotten on the green. Barely. For all his bragging about his golf game, Don was in third place, only ahead of Jake. That's what happened in the presence of a real golfer—everybody else fell apart.

The fairway before Ben was an easy one. A par three—a mere one hundred fifty yards. He pulled the nine iron out of his bag.

"Watch this and weep." Ben wagged his head.

Don and Jake rolled their eyes.

Ben shifted his feet into place and worked a perfect grip on the club. *Keep the head down, stroke through the ball.* He swung forward and connected with a hard, precise *thwack*. The little white circle sailed into blue sky. Ben held the brim of his hat, following its flight. It arched up with precision, then started to fall. "Hah, look at that!"

The ball landed five feet from the hole and rolled forward a little.

Ben raised his fist in the air. "What'd I tell ya!"

"Good one, Ben." Dad gazed at the green with admiration. "A real beauty."

"Not that far from a hole-in-one. 'Course on such a short hole, it wouldn't mean much." Jake laughed and tried to swagger, which didn't work too well. His skinny bowed legs stuck out from his blue shorts like a crane's. Jake pushed his wire-rim glasses back up his nose. He was sweating so much the things wanted to fall off.

"Don't matter how close it was." Don pointed at Ben. "You either make a hole-in-one—or you don't."

Ben raised his chin. "If anybody here's headed for one of those, it's me."

"I bet you get there, Son." His dad slapped a hand on Ben's shoulder.

They climbed into their carts, Ben with his dad, Don and Jake in the second, and took off toward the green. Ben's dad drove their cart. Syton Dearing always liked to be behind the wheel.

"How's Christina this mornin'?" He slowed for a turn on the path.

"Seems okay."

"Better after your talk last night?"

"I don't know. I guess. She still doesn't ... she keeps a lot of things to herself. Now that I know she tends to hide negative stuff, I have to work to figure her out."

"Well, she's with your mama so she's probably havin' a good day."

Yup. No easier person to be with than Ruth Dearing.

His dad threw him a glance. "And how are *you?*"

Ben took a deep breath. "Better. Sleep always helps. I think Christina and I can do this. I *know* we can."

"I'm sure you can too."

They rode the rest of the way in comfortable silence. But there was so much Ben could say. Sometimes he wished he could open up his dad's head and pour out all the wisdom. Especially now that Ben faced marriage, which seemed wonderful and exciting and scary all at once.

There was a time—when Ben was a teenager— he'd thought his parents didn't know much at all. They'd grown up in a different generation, were old-fashioned in many ways. What did they know about being a teenager in today's world? Not until Ben had gone to college had he slowly begun to realize how much his parents *did* know. That their old-fashioned values stood for something. That they were caring and smart, and he couldn't have asked for better parents. He'd started opening up to them more after he graduated college, especially his dad. Then they could talk business, something Ben was learning about firsthand. During one of their talks his father had admitted how much he'd hoped Ben would follow in his footsteps and run the family's Ford dealership some day. Yet he'd never pushed Ben, giving him the chance to choose what he wanted. Took a strong man to let his son follow his own path like that. Made Ben respect him all the more.

They reached the green and climbed out. Don had to go to the edge to hit his ball. Guy took forever getting into position, shifting his feet and wiggling his butt.

Ben put his hand on his hips. "Are you dancin' or playin' golf?"

"Why, you wanna cha-cha?" Don looked up, then back to the ball. "Drat. Now I lost my concentration."

"Come on, Don, we'll be here all day." Jake raised both hands. "Party behind us is gonna get ticked."

Don glanced up the course. "They're way back there."

"Not anymore, they're not."

"Would you be quiet? I can *not* focus with all this chatter."

Ben tried not to laugh. That was the trouble with Don and golf. He was pretty good, but he worked at it too hard. Got all tense. Pulled up his head too soon a lot of times, which made him hit the top of the ball. Ben just let things flow. Plus, Don hated to lose. Now that Ben was here, he was the underdog. And he just couldn't stand it.

"Okay." Dad raised his hands, palms out. "Everybody be still and don't breathe. Don's about to take his shot."

They fell silent, watching Don. He started his butt/foot shuffle again.

"Sometime next Sunday," Dad added.

Jake choked out a laugh. Ben guffawed.

134

Don straightened with a huff. "What's the matter with you people, can't you let a guy hit the ball?"

"No one's stoppin' ya." Dad's eyes twinkled.

"I can't play with all the noise."

"Maybe you just can't play," Ben put in.

Jake looked over his shoulder. "Uh-oh. Party's at the second hole. Better hurry, Don."

"Don't rush me." Don made a frustrated sound in his throat and repositioned his club. Started his shuffle all over again. Ben and his dad exchanged a grin. Ben made a cutting gesture across his throat with one finger. Finally Don's putter connected with the ball. It bounced and rolled straight toward the hole. Whoa.

The ball reached the hole and dropped in.

"Ahhhh!" Don jumped off the ground, putter still in his hand. "See there!" He'd moved to second place.

"Good one, Don." Dad sounded surprised.

"A lucky shot." Ben waved his hand. In his head, he calculated. After he made his next shot—which he would—he'd be only one ahead of Don.

"Call it what you want, it's a par two on a par three hole." Don slid the club into his bag with finesse.

"No more than I'm gonna get," Ben said.

"It's never over till the fat lady sings."

"Who you callin' fat?" Dad felt around his waist.

"Who you callin' a lady?" Jake pretended to be indignant.

Ben's dad and Jake each ended up with one over par. Ben easily knocked his ball in the hole. He retrieved it and pointed at Don. "Still one ahead of you."

"I'll catch up."

"In your next life."

Jake laughed as he headed for his cart. "What's better than a pleasant golf game with family?"

"Nothin'." Dad smiled. "Except winnin'. Not that I know how that feels."

Ben climbed back into the golf cart. He was on a roll. Only three holes, but he could feel it. King of the world today, that was for sure.

Dad was right, Christina was probably having as good a time as he was. She'd be getting to know the women in the family better. Starting to fit in.

They still needed to get a wedding date on the calendar. Should do that tonight at supper.

Wow. Ben smiled to himself. By the time he hit the pillow tonight, he'd know the day he would become Christina's husband. Even in the blazing sun, Ben got goose bumps just thinking about it.

CHAPTER 15

Jess paced her bedroom, going from furious to teary-eyed and back again. Sometimes she was both at once. She swiped away the tears fast as they came. Men. They were nothing but trouble.

She wished she could lie down and rest. Fall asleep and block out the world. Fat chance. She felt wound up enough to punch a hole in the wall. Only one thing could salvage this rotten day—showing up her sisters by making a bang-up feast of those lobsters.

A feast Tamel would sorely miss. And she'd make sure he heard about it, too.

For half an hour or so she paced and mumbled. Told Tamel off a dozen times. Finally she flopped down on her bed, defeated and spent. Her stomach growled. Who knew why she should be hungry so soon. Except that dealing with Tamel had taken a ton of energy.

Jess pushed to her feet and headed out of the room. With most of the family gone, she'd have first dibs at last night's leftovers.

Still frowning, she went down the stairs and headed back toward the family room. Christina sat on the couch, eyes closed. At the sound of Jess's footsteps, her head snapped up. Her eyes looked red.

Jess stopped. "You okay?"

Christina nodded.

Yeah, right. But if the girl wouldn't talk to her, there wasn't much she could do.

Voices filtered from the far west wing hall. Sarah and Mama were back. Bad timing. Jess was in no mood to answer questions about her ride with Tamel.

As if that wasn't enough, Maddy appeared from the east wing hall, eyes at half mast.

"Heard you had a headache," Jess said. It was the polite thing to say.

"Yeah, it's better." Maddy rubbed her face. "I need some iced tea. Hi, Christina. Kids okay?"

Christina ducked her head. "Yes."

Maddy gave her a long look, then shrugged and headed to the kitchen. Jess followed. Sarah and Mama came in at the same time, carrying bags.

"Any more out there?" Jess asked.

"Nope." Mama plopped her bags down on the counter. "We got it all. Includin' everything on your list for supper."

"Great. I picked up some awesome lobsters."

"So how was Tamel?" Sarah would have to bring him up.

"*Don't* ask."

"Oh, no. What hap—"

"Sarah. Can it."

Sarah held up both hands. "Okay, okay."

"Christina, honey, how you doin'?" Peacemaker Mama with a change of subject. She started taking food out of the sacks.

"Fine." Christina didn't move from the couch.

"Kids treat you okay?"

"Yes." She took a deep breath. "But I—"

"Hi, Mama." Alex sidled into the kitchen, wearing Lacey's pink nightgown.

Maddy tilted her head. "Why're you wearin' that?"

Alex pushed her lips together. "My clothes got dirty."

"How?"

"We were, um … eatin'."

"Eatin' what?"

Alex kept her head down and pointed toward the family room at Christina.

Ben's fiancée scrambled off the couch. "I … they were … I was trying to keep them quiet so they wouldn't wake you." Her words tripped over each other. "I'm so sorry, Mrs.—Mama Ruth. We broke a plate. I cleaned it up, and then I had to wash Alex's clothes."

Mama had stopped her work and was concentrating on Christina, who looked like she faced a firing squad. "Well, honey, that's no matter. Don't you worry about a plate."

"She gave us pie and ice cream." Alex pushed her lips together. "And it got *all over* my clothes."

What a little tattletale. Jess shot her niece a scathing look.

"Pie and ice cream?" Sarah and Maddy repeated in stereo.

139

Christina's face blanched. "I didn't know what to do. They were fighting, and I didn't want Maddy—"

"Honey, don't worry about it." Mama walked over and put her hands on the girl's shoulders. "We shouldn't have left you alone with the kids to begin with. Really, this is no big deal."

"Had to wash Alex's clothes." Suddenly Christina's words registered. A lightning bolt hit Jess in the chest. "You washed her clothes?" She threw the question at Christina.

Christina's head pulled back. She nodded.

"Where? In the kitchen sink?" Jess's voice bent upward. "Tell me you washed 'em out here in the sink."

Christina blinked, her face turning whiter. "No."

Oh, no. No, no, no. "Where'd you wash 'em, then?"

"In the washing machine. I just—"

"Aaaaahhhh!" Jess flung both hands in the air. She whirled and ran toward the west wing, yelling. "No, tell me please, no!"

"Jess, what is it?" Sarah called after her.

Jess kept running. She reached the end of the hallway and thudded into the garage. Veered right and sprinted toward the laundry room. Vaguely she registered multiple pairs of feet behind her. Jess passed the dryer, the washer—and skidded to a halt in front of the large tub sink.

It was spewing bubbles.

"Nno!" Jess leapt forward and slapped some of the bubbles aside. Soapy water filled the sink almost to the rim. "Where are they?" She shoved away more bubbles, trying to see the bottom of the sink. One big wet circle floated up her nose. She sneezed, then fought bubbles some more until she could see the bottom.

Mama, Maddy, Sarah, and Christina pulled up beside Jess, breathing hard. Alex wasn't far behind.

There! Jess's nine once perfect lobsters lurched about in the depths of the soapy water like they were drunk.

"Oh, no." Jess plunged her arm into the sink and yanked out the stopper. The water started to drain with loud sucking sounds.

"What happened, what happened?" Alex stood on her toes to look into the sink.

"My lobsters!" Jess nearly wailed the words. She pulled one out of the suds and held it up. Its rubber banded claws waved weakly, bubbles coming out of every hole and cranny in its body. Thing looked like it had crawled through a car wash.

Alex shrieked and jumped away.

Jess plunged her arm in again and pulled out a second soap-saturated lobster. "No, no. This can't be happeniiiing!"

Christina stood back, eyes wide and body rigid. Sarah had one hand pressed against her mouth.

"How could you not *see* them?" Jess whirled on Christina. "I put 'em in the sink with some water."

Christina shook her head.

"Couldn't you see the washing machine drains into this sink?" Jess wanted to strangle Christina's little neck.

"Now, Jess, she didn't know," Mama said.

Jess raised the two lobsters higher in the air. They were still blowing bubbles. One fell quiet. "No!" She shook both of them hard. "Don't *die!* You cannot *die!*" She jerked them around until their heads flopped back and forth. More bubbles oozed out.

Alex screamed and ran from the room.

141

Maddy exploded in her machine-gun laughter. "Oh, ha-ha-ha-ha!"

Jess's cheeks scorched. "Don't you *dare* laugh, do you know how much these things *cost?*"

"Darlin', it's all right." Mama picked up a third lobster. The sink was now drained, nothing left but half a foot of suds.

Jess dropped one critter and smacked on the faucet. "I gotta rinse 'em off." Fresh water poured into the sink, stirring the bubbles. The lobsters clacked their claws in panic.

Sarah started giggling. Jess threw her a look to kill. Maddy laughed even louder until she and Sarah cackled like hyenas, leaning into each other for support. Like a wild woman, Jess batted down the bubbles. Punched and hit and smacked, all the while yelling to the lobsters they'd be all right, just hang on. Finally every last bubble was gone. She snatched up the weakest-looking lobster and thrust it under a deluge of running water, rinsing it front and back, up and down. Scrubbing it with her fingers. "Come on, come on ..."

Bubbles oozed out.

Christina stood frozen.

Maddy and Sarah howled. Even Mama started chuckling.

Fury sent tears to Jess's eyes. "You won't be laughin' come supper time." She dropped lobster number one and started in on number two.

Pogey scurried in, his bare feet slapping the concrete, and their smell coming with him. "What happened?" He pushed around his mother and skidded to a stop. At the sight of bubbles and lobsters and what he surely thought was a crazed Aunt Jess,

142

his eyes went round. Pogey drew in his mouth, stretching his chubby cheeks. "Oooooh!"

Jess's jaw went tight. "Pogey, don't you say a word, I swear."

Pogey chortled. Jess kicked at him. He jumped back but wouldn't shut up. Soon he was holding his stomach, bent over laughing.

Jess's eyes narrowed to slits. She would massacre him later. Along with her sisters. And she would *enjoy* it.

Lacey ran into the room. "What, what, what!"

Jess flicked a look at the ceiling. "Great, let's just get the whole family in here."

Lacey took one look in the sink and shrieked.

"Come on, Jess." Mama did her best to swallow her laughter. "It's just some lobsters." She picked one up and turned it upside down.

What did she think that would do, drain it?

"A bunch of soapy, poisoned ones!" Jess snatched up number three. This wasn't working. Even the two she'd rinsed off were barely alive. And soap kept coming out of 'em. "What'm I gonna fix for supper now? *What?*"

Christina's mouth creaked open. "I'm … *sorry*. I didn't …"

"Don't you worry, honey." Mama patted Christina on the back. "It'll be fine."

"It's not fine!" Jess rinsed and bathed and scrubbed. Maybe, just maybe the lobsters wouldn't taste like laundry water …

"Ah!" No use. She threw number four down into the sink. The thing landed on top of its fellow critters and slowly rolled over. Jess stuck her lobster-smelling hands in her hair. "I can't *believe* this!"

Christina turned and fled the room.

143

"Oh, dear." Mama hurried after her.

"Wait, Christina!" Lacey ran out.

"Jess, what's the p-problem?" Sarah could barely talk for all her cackling. "Haven't you ever heard of eating soap and lobster?"

"Ha-ha-ha-ha!" Maddy stumbled sideways.

"Get out of here, y'all!" Jess pushed her sisters toward the door. "You too, Pogey! Out, out, *out.*" She herded them all into the garage and slammed the laundry room door. She leaned against it, palms pressed against the wood. Dully she gazed across the room at the sink, hearing the faint *scribble-scrabble* of washed-out sea creatures.

First Tamel and now this. Today had to be the *worst* day of her *entire* life.

Jess tried to force herself back to the sink. But what for? Those lobsters could never be cooked now. Put those things in boiling water, and she'd likely fill the entire house with bubbles.

Just wait till Tamel heard about this. She'd never hear the end of it.

Not that she cared what he did or thought anyway.

"Ooohhh." Jess bent over, her eyes filling with tears. Next thing she knew, she'd slid to the floor, elbows on her bent knees and hands over her face. For the first time since she heard Tamel had walked away from his law career—which meant he'd walked away from *her*—Jess let herself bawl.

144

CHAPTER 16

Christina fled down the west wing hallway, through the kitchen and family area toward her room. Tears nearly blinded her. She could hear Mrs. Dearing calling for her to stop, that everything was okay, and she shouldn't feel bad. Jess was just in one of her moods. They'd figure something else out for supper. Lacey called her name too. As Christina reached the top of the east wing hall, guilt got the best of her. She turned and faced them, one hand gripping the door frame.

"P-please ... I just ... need to be by my...self right now."

Before they could say a word, she pivoted and scurried down the hall. Jumped into the safety of her room and locked the door.

Christina sprawled across the bed and buried her face in the covers. She cried and sobbed, then cried some more until her head pounded and the tears dried up. She'd known this wasn't going to work. But did she have to end up being so humiliated? What had she done right since she'd gotten here? Now she'd cost the whole family a special, expensive supper. Everyone would know about it. Everyone would blame her.

It wasn't fair. Ben shouldn't have left her for so many hours. Didn't he know she was uncomfortable here by herself? If he loved her, if he was going to treat her right like he promised, *why* had he gone to play golf? Last night he'd forced her to tell him things she'd never wanted to say. Yet today that conversation made no difference in his behavior at all.

Plain and simple, Ben might think he loved her, but his actions didn't show it. None of the Dearings needed her. What place could she have in this family? She was still an Ugly Bug, unwanted, unlovable. Always had been, always would be. The sooner she accepted that, the easier her life would turn out—

Someone knocked on the door. Christina stiffened, then raised her head.

The knock came again. "Christina? It's Jess." Her voice sounded thick.

Great. The sister Ben was closest to. The one who liked her least of all.

"I'm sorry, Christina, really. It hadn't been a good day for me, and ... Please don't feel bad. We're already pullin' out meat for supper."

As if one apology could undo Jess's accusations. Christina's hurt went too deep for that.

"Are you in there, Christina?"

She glared at the door. "Yes."

"Will you come out?"

"No." The answer shot out of her mouth before she could stop it. She started to apologize but choked on the words. So what if she'd said what she felt? Wasn't that what Ben wanted her to do? Besides, she was tired of trying to please everybody. Clearly it wasn't working.

Why couldn't they just leave her alone?

"Please?"

"I don't *want* to come out, Jess. I don't want to see *anybody* right now."

A long silence pulsed.

"Fine then, be that way."

What a snotty answer. Anger shot through Christina. As if Jessica Dearing had anything to be ticked about. She, who had a loving family and perfect life. Who'd gone joyriding this morning with a man who obviously loved her while Christina stayed home alone and watched three kids she hardly knew. And one of whom was a spoiled brat.

Christina jumped off the bed and strode to the door. Flung it open. Jess was already walking down the hall. "I'm *sorry* about your lobsters, Jess." The words came out hard. "In case you couldn't tell, I didn't mean to do it."

Jess turned around, surprise, then irritation flattening her face. "You sure don't sound sorry."

"Well, I am."

"Well, good for you."

They narrowed their eyes at each other.

"What's wrong with you?" Jess planted her hands on her hips.

147

"You mean why didn't I see your stupid lobsters in the sink?"

Jess's cheeks reddened. "I mean what's *wrong* with you? Everyone's tried to welcome you into this family, and you just run around like some kicked mouse."

"Am I acting like a mouse now?"

"No, and this is a whole lot scarier."

"Maybe you're just not used to having someone stand up to you."

"Maybe you have *no idea* what you're talking about!"

At the top of the hall behind Jess, Maddy poked her head out of the family room. Her eyes were wide. She must have heard everything. She locked eyes with Christina, then jerked back and disappeared.

Reality hit Christina in the chest. What was she *doing?* She'd spent her entire wretched childhood holding in her rage. Had promised herself never, ever to show it to anyone, especially the man she so desperately loved. Or his family. Now she'd let out the bad Christina—on Ben's sister, no less. In his parents' house.

Christina's shoulders drooped. She flushed hot, then cold. "I'm sorry," she whispered. "I don't know what made me…"

Jess gave her a long look. "Yeah, well, you'd better figure it out. 'Cause you got a mess of fury floatin' around inside you, girl."

Her tone kicked anger back up Christina's spine. She tried to force it down, but it wouldn't budge. "And what exactly would you call what's 'floatin' around' inside of *you?* I've seen the way you treat Tamel."

148

Jess inhaled a sharp breath. "Don't you dare mention Tamel to me."

"It's obvious he's crazy in love with you."

"That's *none* of your business!"

"And how I act is none of yours!"

"It *is* when you're about to marry my brother!" Jess stalked two steps toward Christina. "I will not stand by and watch him get his heart broken again. No one in this family will."

Christina drew her head back, stricken. The last thing she wanted was to hurt Ben. "Why don't you watch *yourself,* Miss Know-It-All."

Jess's body went rigid. She pointed at Christina, her voice low and shaking. "I knew somethin' was off-kilter the minute I saw you. You aren't what you pretend to be. Now you've gone way too far." Her voice hitched. "I will *not* let you destroy my brother."

She pivoted and stomped down the hall. Veered left. Christina heard her pounding up the stairs.

Was that a sob?

Weakly, Christina leaned against the wall. Self-loathing and despair poured over her. She'd done it now. Really done it. Maddy was probably still listening from the family room. She'd go tell Mrs. Dearing and Sarah.

No way could Christina face them now.

She escaped back into the guestroom and relocked the door. Fresh tears spilled out of her eyes, no holding them back. She did *not* want to cry. She snatched up her suitcase in the corner and tossed it on the bed. Started throwing in her clothes and toiletries.

The minute Ben came home they were *leaving.* And if he was too mad to drive her, all the better. She couldn't bear to sit in a car with him for six hours anyway. Couldn't stand to see the pain on his face. She'd failed him completely. Failed herself too. She'd been a fool to believe she could have her fairy tale life.

Tamel would take her to Jackson, wouldn't he? She'd pay for the first plane back to Dallas. Find another job. And she would never, ever see the Dearing family again.

CHAPTER 17

Ruth hovered in the kitchen with Sarah, watching Maddy peek around the corner into the hall. In the sink sat five pounds of hamburger—a last-minute substitute for tonight's supper. The dying lobsters still writhed in the laundry tub. Jess hadn't been able to bring herself to throw them out.

Alex's clothes were now in the dryer. All three kids were in the play room, the door closed. Penny was with them. Ruth didn't want the kids to know … whatever was happening. She could hear the hiss of Christina's and Jess's voices but couldn't make out what they said. Whatever it was—it wasn't friendly.

Ruth's throat had gone so tight it felt raw. How had the day fallen apart like this? The very things she'd worried about Christina were coming true. She couldn't bear to think what that might mean for Ben.

Maddy yanked her head back and hurried toward the kitchen. "Oh, my gosh, they're tearin' each other up out there."

Oh, no. Ruth started for the hall. "I have to stop them."

Sarah grabbed her arm. "No, Mama, don't get in the middle of it."

"But—"

"You'll only make it worse."

Stomping feet came up the hall, then headed upstairs. At the end of the east wing a door closed.

Sarah cocked her head. "Sounds like it's over."

Maddy nodded. "Maybe one of them threw in the flag."

"Towel, Maddy," Sarah said. "Throw in the towel; raise the white flag."

"Whatever."

Ruth put her palms against her cheeks. They felt so hot. "I need to go to Christina."

Sarah shook her head. "You already tried goin' after her once. She didn't want to talk to you. Besides Jess told us she was goin' to apologize to her. Apparently even that didn't work."

"But it's not just Jess. First Penny gets mad at her, then the kids give her a hard time, and a plate breaks—which she's blaming herself for. Then the lobsters, and Jess so mad, and you two laughin'—"

"I know, but just let her be for now," Sarah said. "It'll be easier to talk to her when she's calmed down."

"Then I should go talk to Jess. She's upset too."

"Mama, no. You know how mad *she* can get. Let her blow it off."

Ruth sank into a kitchen chair. "What should we do, then? I feel sorry for your sister after she spent all that money. And I can't have Christina bein' so upset. She's our guest."

Maddy looked to Sarah. "We should apologize to Christina too. Even though we were laughin' at Jess, not her." A giggle popped out of Maddy. "It's still funny."

"Yeah, but Christina doesn't seem to understand our humor." Sarah gazed toward the east wing. "She's been so quiet and tryin' to please everybody. But this sure took her over the edge. What if she goes off on Ben like that?"

Maddy sighed. "Not good."

"Now wait, you two." Ruth made eye contact with both her daughters. "You've had issues with your own husbands. Remember how hard it was at first? There's so much to work out between two people. It was the same for your dad and me."

"Oh, come on, Mama," Sarah said, "you and Daddy never had a fight in your life."

"Not for years, maybe, but we did at first."

They fell silent. Ruth thought of the lobsters. She needed to throw them out before they died and stunk up the whole house. Pogey's feet couldn't even compete with that.

She smacked the table. "I've been wantin' new plumbin' for that washin' machine for years. We should have a proper drain, not goin' through that old sink."

Sarah nodded. "I'm sure a certain bunch of lobsters would agree with you."

Maddy chortled. Ruth shot her a look, and she cut the laugh short. Putting on a serious expression,

153

Maddy leaned forward, listening. "Do you hear anything from either of 'em?"

Sarah shook her head.

Maddy drummed her fingers on the counter. "I'm gonna listen at the doors, see what's goin' on." She scurried off.

Ruth rubbed her forehead, picturing Ben on the golf course. How long before the men got home?

"Why's Jess got her knickers in such a twist anyway?" Sarah leaned against the counter. "I mean, I get that the lobsters were expensive, but this is ridiculous."

Ruth stared at the table. "She was with Tamel this morning. I wonder if somethin' went wrong."

"She's been actin' terrible toward him. When's she gonna come off that?"

Ruth shook her head. Her youngest daughter was a complicated woman.

Maddy returned. She shook her head — *not good.*

Sarah stared at her. "What?"

"Jess is up in her room, bawlin'. She wouldn't open the door for me. Christina's in *her* room, cryin'. I didn't even try to get her to come out."

Oh, no. Ruth lowered her head.

"Why is Jess cryin', you think?" Maddy asked Sarah.

"Maybe Tamel?"

"Oh." Maddy thought that over. "Maybe."

Ruth closed her eyes. *Lord, send your peace. Help me know what to do here.*

She stood up. She had to fix this. "I'm goin' to talk to Jess." Her tone said she'd made up her mind. Sarah and Maddy didn't try to stop her.

Ruth hurried up the stairs and knocked lightly on Jess's door. "Sweetie, can I come in?"

"Not now, Mama, please." Jess's words sounded clogged.

"I'm worried about you. Don't want you feelin' bad up here by yourself."

"I'll be okay."

She didn't sound okay at all. And this was definitely more than a bunch of soapy lobsters. "Please, Jess. Tell me what's wrong."

"I don't want to talk right now." Jess let out a sob. "Just ... give me a while, okay?"

Ruth lingered at the door, her heart in knots. Wanting to make everything all right for her daughter, knowing she couldn't. "Okay, honey. I'll be downstairs when you need me."

She descended the steps slowly, hesitated at the top of the east wing hall, then walked toward Christina's room. At the door, she listened.

No sound.

"Christina?" She knocked.

No answer. Then—"I'm sleeping."

Christina's tone clearly said she didn't want to be bothered.

Ruth winced. "Okay."

She returned to the kitchen and the questioning gazes of her two older daughters. Sarah raised her eyebrows. "Well?"

Ruth shook her head.

She lowered herself into a kitchen chair and stared out the window. She just couldn't sit back and do nothing. After a moment she straightened. "I'm gonna call Ben and Tamel. They're the only two who can straighten this out."

Sarah looked at her askance. "I'm not sure that's a good idea."

"You have a better one?"

"Just let them work this out, Mama," Maddy said. "You can't fix everything."

"Well, I can try." Besides, Ruth knew human nature. Christina and Jess might be mad at first that she'd made the calls. But the sooner these two talked things out with the men in their lives, the better it would be—for the whole family. "I'll have to do this carefully, though. If Ben lights into Jess for upsetting Christina ..."

Maddy pursed her lips. "Oh, boy."

Ruth got up and reached for the phone.

CHAPTER 18

Tamel hadn't known what to do with himself ever since he got home. He'd stomped around the house, then the backyard. Fortunately his dad had been taking a nap. When Henry Curd did wake up, he was no help. He gimped out of his room, one hand at his back, working hard to breathe. White hair stuck up on one side of his head. His wrinkles looked deeper than Tamel had ever seen them. Maybe he wouldn't even last a year.

The thought pierced.

"What's the matter with you?" Tamel's dad asked after one look at his face.

Tamel turned away. "I just got things on my mind."

A moment of silence. "You worried about the business? It's all right, Son, somebody'll die soon, you'll see. We'll get some money comin' in."

Tamel closed his eyes. He'd laugh if it wasn't so grim. His dad had no business working at all. He could hardly stand long enough to do the embalming anymore. Which Tamel knew nothing about. And his dad had stopped doing the books for the funeral parlor long ago. Tamel had completely taken over the accounting and taxes.

He turned back toward his father, seeing the gray face. "You need to sit down. I'll get you some water."

His father shuffled over to his favorite chair in front of the TV. "That'd be good."

It was the closest to a *thank-you* Tamel would ever get.

He poured a glass of water over ice and placed it on the table beside his father's chair. "I'm gonna go out and sit on the porch awhile."

"Awful hot out there."

Tamel shrugged.

Seated outside, he stared at the weedy lawn and cracked driveway. What was he doing here? Other than going crazy. He longed for the life he knew, working in the law firm, using the knowledge he'd slaved so long to acquire. Here every day went by like molasses, slow-poured and dark.

Until Jess visited. Those were the few bright moments.

Tamel dropped his head. After tomorrow she'd be gone again. And this time he wasn't sure if she'd even want to see him when she returned.

Her judgment of him cut deep. Took him all the way back to high school when he thought he'd never measure up to her. He was laid back and easy; she was dynamic and driven. Her personality was far better suited to law than his. Yet he'd found fulfillment in it too. In large part because they were both on parallel roads.

Tamel's cell rang, jarring him from his thoughts. He pulled it from his back pocket and read the ID. *Syton Dearing.* His heart lurched. Jess, calling from her parents' phone?

"Hello?" He leaned forward in his chair.

"Tamel, it's Mama Ruth."

She sounded upset. That realization chased away his disappointment. His back straightened. "Something wrong?"

"It's Jess. She's locked up in her room, cryin' her eyes out. Won't come out for anybody."

Crying? A tinge of hope glimmered inside him. "Why?"

"Well, one reason is soapy lobsters."

"Huh?"

Mama Ruth told him the "short version" of a crazy tale involving Jess's lobsters, dirty clothes, and the large sink the washing machine drained into. "I'm afraid supper's ruined. Jess was so lookin' forward to cookin' for us."

Tamel frowned at the worn wooden floor of the porch. "I see." Which he didn't.

"But I don't think that's all. I was wonderin'—did somethin' happen between you two this mornin'?"

He hesitated. "Why?"

"You don't have to tell me what it was. I just ... Jess is cryin' way too long over a silly thing like lobsters. So if you think it's got somethin' to do with you, I wonder if you'd come over. Try to talk to her."

The hope inside Tamel glowed stronger. He hadn't dared think Jess was hurting too. If she was hurting she had to *care.*

159

But she was also mad as a wet panther. The feeling inside him flickered. His going over there could make things worse.

"Please, Tamel. I've got Jess in one room and Christina in another ..."

"What's wrong with Christina?"

"She argued with Jess. But that was after the lobsters, and the apple pie and ice cream, and the broken plate. And Penny."

Tamel didn't even want to ask.

"It's just a total mess over here. Never had such a thing happen durin' a family reunion—" Her voice caught.

That brought Tamel to his feet. He'd do anything to help Mama Ruth. "I'll be right there."

He clicked off the phone and hurried into the house for his car keys.

CHAPTER 19

At twelve-forty Ben and the rest of his foursome
were on the green at the thirteenth hole. The
afternoon was hotter than a billy goat in a pepper
patch. But Ben had been playing great—ahead of the
others by five strokes. This game was in the bag.

Ben's cell phone rang. It was Mama, sounding
very worried. "Christina's all upset and won't talk to
any of us. She's holed up in her room, just won't
come out. I think you should come home."

Oh, no. Ben's nerves prickled. "What happened?"

Dad caught the concern in his voice and shot him
a silent question—*something wrong?*

Mama launched into a long explanation that
started with Penny howling and ended with an
argument between Christina and Jess. Ben stared
down the course toward the fourteenth hole, his
mouth open.

"Jess *argued* with Christina?" After he'd warned his sister? Anger wrapped around his chest. He'd strangle her.

"Well, she did get a little carried away over the lobsters. But actually"—Mama hesitated—"she tried to apologize. Sounds like Christina wouldn't accept it."

What? Christina bent over backwards to please everybody. Something was seriously wrong here. "How did all this happen in just a few hours?"

"I'm wonderin' that myself. It's partially my fault. Sarah and I went to the store and left Christina with the kids."

"Where was Maddy?"

"In her room with a headache."

Ben's dad still focused on his face. "Sounds like somethin's goin' on at home," Dad said in a low voice to Jake.

Wait. Everybody had scattered, leaving Christina to babysit? She was way too hard on herself to be left like that. One little thing going wrong, and she'd drown in self-blame.

So why had *he* left her?

The thought hit Ben in the gut. Last night's conversation with Christina came rushing back. She didn't want to be expected to serve him. Didn't want to be taken for granted. He'd promised not to do those things. Promised to take care of her the way she wanted. He'd already failed.

But golf with the men in his family was so important. It was *tradition*.

"Ben, you there?"

He put a hand over his eyes. "Yeah. We'll come home. It'll take about half an hour to get there. We'll hurry." He punched off the call.

"What happened?" his dad asked.

"More like what didn't." Ben wiped sweat off his temple. Why was it that ever since he and Christina had gotten to Justus, things started going bad? "We need to go right now. I never should have left Christina." He walked over and yanked up his ball.

This was just terrific, coming after last night's argument. Christina had been hard enough to deal with then. Now practically the whole family was involved. She was surely thinking they were all against her.

What was he going to have to do to make her happy?

CHAPTER 20

Jess slumped on her bed, spent from crying and thoroughly ticked at herself. What in the world was wrong with her? She couldn't remember bawling like that in years. Just because she'd probably ruined her brother's engagement. But so what? Clearly, Ben could do a whole lot better than Christina Day anyway. Jess knew good and well what Granddad Pete would say about their relationship if he was still alive. *"That dog won't hunt."* And Jess was far from ready to forgive Christina for the things she'd said. Like she could just barge into this family and attack one of Ben's sisters.

As for crying over Tamel, he was hardly worth it.

Jess ran a hand over her face. In a couple days she'd be back in Memphis and at work. Life would cycle back to seventy-hour weeks at the office. She wouldn't have time to think about Tamel Curd.

A knock sounded on her door. Jess shot a dark look in its direction. Why couldn't they just leave her alone? *"What?"*

"It's Tamel."

Tamel? Jess jerked up straight. Her legs started to bounce her off the bed, toward the door—

Wait a minute. No, no, no. What did he expect— to argue some more on her own turf? Jess's fingers dug into the bedcovers. "What do *you* want?"

"Let me in."

"You're crazy, Tamel Curd, comin' here. I don't want to talk to you."

"Let me in, Jess." He rattled the knob.

"Go away."

"You don't let me in, I'm breakin' this door down."

"Oh, that'll be real nice. Mama will love the new look."

"Have it your way."

Jess heard him back up, like he was ready to take a running leap. He could not be serious. She shot off the bed and flung open the door. Tamel stood there with his arms crossed, as if he knew that's what she'd do. Jess's cheeks flushed. "You—" She moved to slam the door, but Tamel pushed his way into her room and shut it behind him.

They faced off a mere two feet apart, Jess breathing hard, Tamel's jaw tight.

"Get out." She tried to yank the door open, but his hand pressed against it.

"You know you want me here."

"Do not."

"Then why're you in here cryin'?"

"Do I *look* like I'm cryin'?

"You look like you have been."

"You need your eyes fixed."

Tamel drew back, his fingers flexing. Emotions scuttled across his face like blown sand over wood.

In a split second he closed the space between them, planted his hands on her cheeks, and kissed her. Hard.

Jess stiffened in pure shock. Her palms rose, ready to push him off ... not able to do it. She felt his breath on her face, his lips on hers—and her heart shimmied. She didn't want it to end. Should never have let it begin. She grasped Tamel's shoulders to shove him away. He wrapped his arms around her. Jess's muscles locked tighter ... then melted. Before she could stop herself her hands had slipped around his back, her mouth responding.

Oh, have mercy.

Tamel wound his fingers in her hair. Jess could feel his wild heartbeat against hers. His kiss didn't get any gentler, and she didn't want it to.

After forever—or was it mere seconds?—Tamel pulled away, his face still close to hers. He grinned, showing his dimples. "You're not cryin' now."

Jess stepped back, her nerves fiery. What had she done? "Get away from me, Tamel."

He let his arms fall, his expression turning serious. For a long moment he gazed at her. Jess's heart flopped over. "Please talk to me."

How dare he do this, after he'd let her know their lives would never connect? Jess felt her face go hot. "I have nothin' to say to you."

He reached for her hands. She yanked them away. He followed their movement and caught her by the wrists. "Jess, I'm not leavin'."

"This is *my* room, Tamel. You can just get out."

"No, I can't."

"And why is that?"

"Because I love you."

The words soared through her. Then stabbed her in the chest. She stared at him, not finding a thing to say. Her throat tightened, and she swallowed hard. Slowly, her spine straightened.

"That's just great, Tamel, what do you expect me to do about it?"

"Love me back."

She snorted. "For what? I'm workin' my tail off as a lawyer in Memphis, remember? You're lookin' at stayin' in Justus the rest of your life."

"I never said I was stayin' in Justus forever."

"You most certainly did."

"No, I didn't. 'Cause I'm not. You just assumed I was."

"I did not assume. You *told* me so!"

"Think back, Jess, remember our conversation. At what point did I tell you I'm stayin'?"

Her mouth opened, their argument running through her head. *"Is that a yes? You're gonna stay?"*

"I'd be the same person."

Jess's mouth closed. She pulled her hands away from his grasp. What kind of game was he playing? "Why'd you do that, why didn't you answer me straight?"

"Because I want you to love *me*, not my career."

She jerked her head back. "Who said I love *anything* about you, Tamel Curd?"

"Jess." Pain flicked across his face. "Stop."

She looked away, stricken. Why on earth did she want him to kiss her again? She wanted just as much to smack him. Send him reeling across the room.

"Tamel." She fought to keep her voice from trembling. "You purposely let me think you plan to stay here and run a funeral parlor the rest of your life. You let me think we have no future." Tears bit her eyes. She tried to blink them back.

"I wanted t—"

"Fine! You think I was cryin'? Maybe I was. And maybe it was about you. Happy now?"

"I ..." He shook his head.

"Oh, for once you have nothin' to say." Jess pressed her lips together. "Why did you hurt me like that? Why didn't you just *talk* to me?"

"I'm sorry."

"You should be." A tear fell onto her cheek. She whisked it away.

Tamel caught one of her hands again. "Can we just ... let's sit down."

She shrugged. Let him lead her to the foot of the bed. They sat.

Jess crossed her arms and glared at the carpet.

"Listen to me." Tamel clasped his hands in his lap, clearly struggling for words. "I thought you were lookin' down on me because I'm not workin' as an attorney right now. I wanted you to see I'm still *me*. I'm the guy you grew up with. The one who's always been your friend and there for you. Who got to take you to the prom our junior year—most wonderful day of my life. The guy who's loved you since ninth grade."

Ninth grade? Jess's eyes widened, but she kept her gaze on the floor.

"The romantic part of me wanted to hear you say you'd be with me wherever I was. Whatever I did. That you cared for me no matter what."

Jess closed her eyes and felt another tear fall. It plopped on her shorts. She waited for Tamel to say more, but he fell silent.

"That wasn't fair." She rubbed at the tear stain with her knuckles. "Because you're talkin' two different things. You say you'd be the same person, no matter your job. Yes, you would. And you're a wonderful person. But I have a life I've struggled to achieve. I just couldn't imagine livin' in this small town forever—even if I did grow up here. I love bein' in a big city. Love the energy and flow of it." The rest poured out of her, no holding it back. Oh, would she regret it. "I always thought one day you'd be in the same city with me. Even though we'd never said it. Even though we'd danced around it—I knew. And I knew you did, too."

She dared a glance at him. He was gazing at her with wonder. Jess pulled in her top lip. Focused again on her lap.

"So then—suddenly—you change everything. You decide to move here, without tellin' me first. Then you decide to *stay* here—as far as I can see. Also without any discussion. And you've still never really *said* anything about carin' for me. So what am I left to think? That clearly I was wrong. That you don't care what I feel at all—" Her voice squeezed off. Oh, good grief, why couldn't she just hold it together? She cinched her eyes shut.

"Jess." Tamel put his arm around her shoulder and pulled her close. She didn't resist. "I've done nothin' but care about you for years."

That did it. More tears came. Jess hiccupped and pressed a fist to her mouth. Tamel let her sniffle, rubbing the side of her head. His touch was so gentle it made her cry all the harder. Drat it all.

Finally she took a deep, shuddering breath. Wiped her face and sat up. She winced. "Oh, my head hurts."

170

"Happens when you're in the presence of greatness."

Jess threw him a weary look. He tipped his head in an apology.

Next thing she knew, he was kissing her again. How did that even happen? She told herself to pull back, but not a single muscle listened. The kiss was long and slow, and the best thing she ever tasted in her life. When they finally parted Jess felt utterly spent.

Self-consciousness bloomed inside her. What were they supposed to do now? She focused across the room, lacing and unlacing her fingers. This would totally complicate everything. How could she focus on her career with Tamel on her mind? She wasn't *supposed* to have a man in her life.

Plus, no way was she giving her sisters the satisfaction of seeing her smitten.

"Jess."

"Hmm."

"Wanna tell me somethin'?"

She only had a million thoughts on her mind. "What?"

"You know."

Her fingers stilled. Fear wound up her spine. Maybe this was all wrong. She should just get up and walk away, end it before it got any further.

Tamel put his fingers beneath her chin and turned her face toward his. "Go on. Say it."

She lowered her gaze, feeling the heat of his touch.

"It won't kill you, you know."

It just might.

"Do I have to kiss you again?"

"Oh, like that's a real chore?"

171

"Well, you didn't make the first one exactly easy."
She smiled in spite of herself.

Tamel smiled back. His dimples creased—so cute.
She could look at them all day. And suddenly she
realized how much she'd missed them in Memphis.
Jess found herself gazing down the tracks of her
life—a life without this man who'd been there since
childhood—and they faded into a horizon cold and
empty.

She needed her career. She needed Tamel.

The words bubbled up inside Jess, spilled out of
her mouth. "I love you, Tamel Curd."

She blinked, surprised at herself. The words hung
between them. Part of her wanted to bat them away.

Tamel grinned and wagged his head. "See there.
Told ya."

She flexed her shoulders. "Aren't you the smart
aleck."

"Yup. And *you* don't know as much as you think
you do."

Jess blew out air. "You are totally exasperatin'."

"Not half as bad as you."

"Oh, really."

"Shut up, Jess."

He pulled her close and kissed her again.

CHAPTER 21

Ruth paced the kitchen, tapping a thumb against her chin. What was going on up there? Tamel had been with Jess for some time now.

At least she wasn't hearing any yelling. Or furniture being thrown.

"They'll be fine, Mom, relax." Sarah sat at the table, an afternoon latte before her. She held Penny, who'd apparently had enough of being in the play room with the kids. "Won't they, Lady P." The Yorkie gave her a look as if to say there was no predicting this crazy family. Sarah scratched behind her ears, and Penny stuck her nose forward, basking in her touch.

Maddy was in the laundry room, rescuing Alex's clean clothes from the dryer. Time to get her daughter dressed again. Although the little girl had taken a shine to her cousin's pink nightgown and announced she wanted to wear it all day. "Ain't happenin', chil'," Maddy had told her. "You need to wear real clothes."

And where was Ben? The men should be home any minute now. Christina still hid in her room. Twice Ruth had started to go knock on her door, and twice her daughters had stopped her.

"Ben will be here soon, Mom." Sarah always could read Ruth's thoughts. "You called him home early from his game, isn't that enough?"

None of them had ever interfered with the men's golf before.

"I know, I know, but I need to do *somethin'*." Other than just praying, which she'd been at fervently since phoning Ben and Tamel.

"So go take care of the lobsters."

"Uh-uh. I'm leavin' 'em for Sy. I have no idea what to do. We throw them in our garbage, they'll stink to high heaven. It's not picked up for another two days."

"Maybe we should have a buryin' party."

"Jess would love that."

Maddy was coming down the hall, carrying Alex's clothes. "All right, let's get you dressed." She stepped into the play room.

"Jess is gonna come down here glowin' and holdin' hands with Tamel, you'll see," Sarah said. "She won't care a whit about those lobsters anymore."

"You think so?"

"I know Jess better than she knows herself. She can't fool me."

Ruth kept pacing. Maddy entered the kitchen, holding Lacey's nightgown. She put it on the table before Sarah. "Here you go."

"What, you want *me* to wear it now?"

"You'll look great."

Ruth shook her head. How could they tease at a time like this?

"Did you check in on our lobster friends?" Sarah asked.

Maddy waved her hand. "I purposely did not *even* look. But I heard 'em. They're dyin' a slow death in there."

Lady Penelope jumped daintily off Sarah's lap and headed for her water bowl. Tiny lap-laps sounded across the tile.

"We should get the kids out of that play room." Sarah took a drink of her latte. "Send 'em outside to run around."

"It's too hot." Maddy sat down.

"The men are out there."

"The men are crazy."

Ruth heard the distant grind of the garage door. "They're here!"

"Good." Sarah exchanged a look with her sister. "Now maybe she'll relax."

"You talkin' about *our* mother?"

Ruth hurried down the hall and into the garage to greet the men. They pushed out of the car, tired and sweaty. Ben looked beside himself. She couldn't tell if he was mad or frustrated, or both. "She still in her room?" he asked.

"Yes."

He headed toward the kitchen, on a mission.

Sy's handsome face was red from the sun. "Sounds like you got some girl drama goin' on, Ruthie." With three daughters, he'd seen his share of drama over the years.

175

"More than some." She spilled out the details. Jake and Don listened in. Didn't take long before all three of them were laughing.

"Would you *stop*?" Ruth pressed her palms to her face. "This isn't funny."

The men tried their best to untwist their mouths. Didn't work very well.

"You wouldn't be laughin' if you were in Ben's shoes. He's got a lot to straighten out."

"Boy." Jake pushed up his glasses. "I sure am glad those crazy early relationship days are behind me and Sarah. Near wore me out. It's much easier bein' an old married man."

Sy snorted. "If you're old, what does that make me?"

"Ancient." Jake opened the trunk of the car.

"So where are these lobsters now?" Sy lifted out his golf clubs.

"Still in the sink. You have to get rid of 'em somehow."

"Why don't we eat 'em?"

"They're full of soap!"

Sy shrugged. "They'll be good and clean." Jake and Don laughed.

Oh, honestly.

Sy stowed his golf clubs in the back corner of the garage. "Okay, lady of mine, let's take a look at that sink full of dyin' critters."

"I got to see this, too." Don set down his clubs and headed for the washing machine. Jake followed.

"You comin'?" Sy turned to Ruth.

"I've seen enough of 'em. Just ... do somethin' about it, okay?"

Her husband saluted. "Syton Dearing to the rescue, ma'am." He headed off behind his sons-in-law.

"And don't go teasin' Jess when you see her!" Ruth called after them. "She's been through enough. Don't tease her about Tamel, either."

"That's a lot to ask." Jake snickered to Don.

"Way too much." They disappeared into the laundry room.

Ruth stood in the garage, bouncing a fist against her hip. What more could she do now?

She lowered her head and stared at the concrete floor. *Dear Lord, please get my family through the rest of this day.*

CHAPTER 22

Christina heard a knock on her bedroom door. Her nerves spritzed. How many times did she have to say she didn't want to talk to anyone?

"Christina, it's Ben."

Ben! She checked her watch. He shouldn't be back for at least another hour.

"Let me in."

She had to look a sight. All that crying and makeup smeared. She jumped from the bed and checked herself in the mirror. Ran both hands through her hair.

With a deep breath, she opened the door.

Ben looked down at her, worry creasing his forehead. He was sunburned and sweaty, and she couldn't read his expression.

He was probably really ticked at her.

He came into the room and closed the door. Kept gazing at her, as if she might melt through the floor any minute.

"What happened?"

"Why are you back so early?"

"Mom called me. What happened?"

Tears pricked Christina's eyes. She turned away. "Everything."

Ben took her hand. Sat her down on the gold-padded bench against the wall. He settled beside her. "Tell me."

Where to begin? She'd alienated everyone in the family, starting with the dog. She'd ruined a very expensive meal. She'd argued with Jess—when Jess was trying to apologize. There was no going back on any of it now.

"You can't fix this, Ben. I know you think you can fix everything, but ..." She raised a hand.

He was silent for a moment. "You're right. *You're* gonna have to do some of it."

"I *can't*."

"Sure you can. I'll be there beside you."

Christina shook her head. She didn't know how to even face the family again, much less make things right. "I've done everything wrong. They don't like me."

"That's not true. It's all in your head."

She pictured Jess's face as they argued, the rigidness of her body. Her cutting tone. "Jess does *not* like me."

Ben sighed. "First you have to tell me what happened."

"Didn't your mom tell you anything?"

"I want to hear it from *you*."

Oh. So they *had* been talking about her.

180

Then what was the point of going over it again? She didn't want to hear the words from her own mouth. They would all sound so silly.

"Come on, Christina."

She heaved a sigh.

Head down, she told him. Everything. By the time she was done her mouth was dry. And she felt more stupid than ever. How had she let all that happen? She should have just stood up to bratty Alex.

"I'm so sorry." Ben patted her leg. "I never should have left you."

"It's not your fault."

"It is. If I'd been here none of this would have happened."

Maybe so, but she couldn't blame him. All of the anger that had popped out of her last night and this afternoon seemed to have drained away. She couldn't find the tiniest bit left inside her.

Was it gone for good?

Maybe she was just too worn out to feel it.

"Please forgive me for leavin' you." Ben put an arm around her. She tensed at his touch. "Last night I promised not to ask too much of you. And I already failed."

She still couldn't look at him. "There's nothing to forgive."

Ben rubbed her shoulder.

"Okay, then." His tone lightened. "Let's get out of this room and join the family."

Sure.

"Except I need to take a shower first. We'll have somethin' else to eat tonight. Everybody will be just fine."

181

Christina stared at the carpet. She wasn't just fine. Couldn't he see that? "I want you to take me home, Ben."

He stilled. "I am takin' you home — on Monday."

"I want to leave now."

"*What?*"

She nodded.

"Why?"

What did she have to do, lay it all out for him? No matter how much they tried to love each other, they were just too different. She didn't understand him; he didn't understand her. They never would.

"I'm not takin' you home." Ben's voice firmed. "You can't run away from this. It would just leave everything hangin', and you'd have to fix it later."

"Don't you get it?" She twisted to face him. "I can't be a part of your family!"

Ben blinked, shock creasing his face. "What do you mean? Of course you can."

Christina looked away, closed her eyes. "No. I can't."

She could hear him breathing.

Ben took his arm away from her shoulders. "I don't get it. Why are you doing this?"

She couldn't reply.

He thumped the side of the bench. "You said you loved me."

"I do." Her heart wanted to bend in two.

"And I love you. So ... what's the problem?"

"Sometimes love's not enough."

"It's *always* enough."

She rubbed a thumb over her fingers. "Don't you see? There's too much difference between you and me. I don't ... I don't know how to do this."

"Do what, be at a family reunion?"

182

"Be with *you*, Ben. Because you're so much a part of them."

He gazed at her, incredulous. "You don't want to be with me?"

"I do, but ... it won't work."

"So ... what then? You tellin' me you want to break our engagement?"

He had to know that's what she was saying. That it was over between them. It had to be. Because she would never come between him and his family, not that she'd succeed if she tried. "You know I don't fit here."

"Of course you do. Because you fit with *me.*"

She gave her head a tiny shake.

"Okay, then, Christina, where *do* you fit?"

She hesitated, then shrugged.

"Come on, that deserves an answer. Where do you fit? Back in your parents' house?"

Her fingers dug into the bench's cushion. How could he even say that?

"Or maybe at work, goin' home each night alone? Where you sit and think about your wretched childhood?"

Pain exploded in Christina's lungs. She held back a sob.

"Because that's all you had before we got together. And it's all you'll have again without me — your awful memories of parents so horrible I could strangle them with my bare hands. You want to wallow in that the rest of your life, Christina? Is that what you want?"

That wasn't fair. "If I did, I wouldn't have ever let you take me out."

"But now you want to return to it? To your bruised life, alone?"

"I ... no."

Ben raised his hands. "Then *what* are we talkin' about?"

Christina pushed to her feet. Some of the anger she couldn't find a minute ago now trickled through her. Why did he have to make this so hard?

"I *don't* fit with your family! I don't have any idea how to be in a close, big group like them. It's so far from my childhood, you can't even imagine."

"I know." Ben's expression softened. He leaned forward to reach for her, but she stepped back.

His hands fell to his lap, his eyes glazing with tears. "Don't pull away from me. Please."

Her own eyes filled again. "We can't be together, Ben. It just won't work. I'll never measure up. So we might as well stop now."

"Of course you measure up. You're more than I ever dreamed of."

Her tears fell. But she shook her head. "Take me home. Please."

A mask of pain pulled over Ben's face. He stood. "I'm not takin' you." His chin quivered, even as he spit out the words. "I'm gonna let you sit right here, in this room. You want to stay here all tonight and tomorrow and pout about what a sorry person you are, be my guest. We want you out there with us, *part* of us, me especially. But I can't force you. Nobody can do this but *you*."

Christina's eyes locked with Ben's, unable to tear away. She swallowed, and it hurt her throat.

"Here's what it comes down to, Christina. Are you gonna let your awful past ruin the rest of your life? Or are you willin' to do the work to climb out of it? Build a new future? Because that future belongs with *me*." He poked himself in the chest. "Nobody

184

else is gonna love you like I do. No other family will love you like this one—if you'll just let 'em. If you'll quit pushin' everyone away." He swung away from her, then reeled back. "You keep talkin' about how you're not good enough. Truth is, you act like you're *too* good. That you're beyond my love, my family's acceptance. That's an arrogance all its own. You wanna spend the rest of your life with that kind of attitude, go right ahead. But you'll be miserable. And you'll *deserve* it!"

Ben pushed past her and flung open the door. Strode through it and closed it hard without looking back. Christina heard his heavy footsteps fade down the hall.

She stared at the door, stunned.

The hurt inside her burst open, and her legs went weak. Christina threw herself on the bed and cried.

CHAPTER 23

Ruth stood in an assembly line at the kitchen counter with Maddy and Sarah, putting together ham sandwiches for a late lunch. She already had potato salad made, and they'd pulled out a large bag of chips from the pantry. Lunch at Dearing reunions tended to be chaotic, folks eating whenever they had the chance. But now that the men had come home early, the family would end up eating together around the dining room table.

Except maybe Ben and Christina. And Jess and Tamel.

She threw a glance across the family room, ever on the watch for any of those four to appear.

Somewhere far down the east wing a door slammed. Ruth stilled.

Hard footsteps stomped up the hall. Had to be Ben.

Slices of ham still in her hand, Ruth hurried through the family room and toward the front hall. Her son was near the top of the stairs.

"Ben!"

He turned, his face taut with anger.

"What happened?"

"I can't talk right now." He swiveled and disappeared on the second floor.

Air rushed from Ruth's lungs.

Heavy-hearted, she made her way back to the kitchen. Maddy and Sarah raised their eyebrows in silent questions. Ruth shook her head. "Looks like now *they're* fightin'."

"Oh, boy." Sarah looked at the line-up of sandwiches. "Guess we'd better make two less."

"What about Jess?" Maddy held a knife and a jar of mayonnaise. "And should we make one for Tamel?"

"Tamel always wants to eat." Sarah laid cheese on a slice of bread.

"Yeah, but Jess might not want him to stay."

"Jess doesn't know what she wants. That's the problem."

Ruth laid the ham slices on a plate and rinsed her hands. Her thoughts still snagged on Ben and Christina. "How can you two be talkin' about the food at a time like this?"

Sarah put cheese on another sandwich. "Don't worry, Mama, if it's meant to be, they'll work it out."

What if it wasn't meant to be? Ben would be devastated.

"As for Jess, she's so stubborn," Sarah said. "If she doesn't see the light during this visit, it'll be a while before she gets back here. She could lose Tamel altogether. Then she'll be sorry."

"Yeah," Maddy said, "cute as he is, other women'll flock to him like geese to honey."

Sarah snickered. "Bees to honey."

"What?"

"*Bees*, Maddy."

Maddy screwed up her face. "Bees don't flock."

"But they—" Sarah raised both hands. "Oh, never mind."

Voices sounded in the front hallway. *Jess!* Ruth's heart wavered. "Here they come," she whispered. "Now, don't you two say anything."

Sarah put on an innocent face. "Who, us?"

All three heads swung toward the family room doorway. Ruth could feel the questions vibrating off Maddy and Sarah.

Jess came through the entrance, followed by Tamel.

"Hi, you two." Ruth searched Jess's face. Her daughter held her head high, as if trying to appear nonchalant, even as three pairs of eyes looked her over. All the same, Jess's expression seemed ... softer. "You hungry? We're makin' sandwiches. Tamel?"

"Sure, thanks, Mama Ruth."

Jess gave a tight smile. "Yeah, me too."

Ruth nodded. Jess looked different beside Tamel. That simmering hurt masked by anger was gone. "You stayin' for supper, Tamel?"

"No, ma'am, I'd love to, but I need to feed my dad. I'll be over after supper, though. Jess and I are goin' out for a while."

Jess threw dagger gazes at Sarah, then Maddy. Daring either of them to say one word.

"Okay." Ruth kept her voice light. "Maybe you can have some dessert with us before y'all go."

189

"That would be great."

Ruth shot up a silent prayer of thanks. She turned back to the sandwich-making. From the corner of her eye she glanced at Sarah, unable to keep her lips from curving. Sarah smiled back.

"Where's Christina and Ben?" Jess asked.

"In their rooms." Ruth sighed. "Things don't look good."

"Oh." Jess studied the counter. "Wonder if I should try to go and apologize again. Although that didn't work so well the first time."

"Maybe you ought to just leave her alone." Sarah put cheese on the last sandwich. "Whatever's goin' on, she and Ben have to work it out."

"She doesn't want to work it out, that's just it. That girl has issues."

"Shh." Ruth shot a look toward the hall. "Keep your voice down."

Jess walked over and laid a hand on her mama's shoulder. "You'd better prepare yourself. I don't think this is gonna work. And in the end Ben will be better off without her."

Ruth would not dwell on that thought. Her son would be crushed. "We just need to give her extra space. She's had a hard life."

"I get that, Mama. But she doesn't seem willin' to *let* us give her extra space. She's just decided that for whatever reason, she can't blend into this family."

"Well." Ruth started putting sandwiches on plates. "We'll see."

Everyone assembled for lunch—except Ben and Christina. Sy, Jake, and Don were showered and smelling fresh as a flower patch. After lunch Sy planned to haul the lobster corpses down to the dumpster behind Piggly Wiggly. They wouldn't sit

190

there long before the bin was emptied. Lady Penelope trotted into the dining room as if she'd never encountered the "family's eating" rule in her life. Sy pointed toward the kitchen and told her to get into her bed. She marched out, nose in the air.

"Where's Christina, I want to sit by her." Lacey looked around.

"In her room, restin'." Sarah patted the place beside her. "Sit here."

"I'll go get her."

"No."

"But—"

"*Sit.*"

Lacey sat.

"I don't care if she's not here." Alex picked up a potato chip. "She got my clothes dirty."

"You did that yourself." Lacey's eyes flashed. "You're the one who spilled your pie."

"She gave it to me."

"You wanted it!"

"Girls." Jake frowned at both of them. "Hush."

"Alex, I don't want to hear you say one more word about Christina." Maddy pointed at her daughter.

"But she—"

"You want to go to your room?" Don gave her a hard look.

Alex pouted and shook her head.

"Then be quiet."

The rest of the meal passed with less than animated conversation between bouts of silence—a first for the Dearings. Ben's seat looked so empty. Ruth could almost feel the concern for him rolling off each person. She exchanged a long, knowing look with Sy down the length of the table. For the first time she let herself wonder if Christina's presence in the family would cause more scenes like this. How would they handle it? And Ben's life could become such a roller coaster.

What if he *was* better off without her?

Ruth could hardly taste her sandwich. There was only so much a mother could do to fix things for her children. When they were little it was much easier. She could kiss the scrapes and bandage the cuts. Nurse them when they were sick. But to stand by and watch an adult child be deeply hurt cut her to the core.

After lunch Tamel left to be with his father. He insisted on dumping the now dead lobsters at Piggly Wiggly for Sy. "No big deal." He shrugged. "I drive a hearse." Maddy and Sarah shooed their kids outside to play in the backyard awhile. Sy and Don said they'd toss them the Frisbee.

Sarah and Jake took off to scour the town for the perfect place to shoot the family summer photo. They happened to walk out the door the same time as Tamel, who was lugging the tied plastic bag of lobsters. They stopped for a minute on the sidewalk and talked. Ruth spotted Jess watching them through the front window, Maddy beside her. She joined them.

"Now what do you suppose they're yakkin' about?" Jess narrowed her eyes at the threesome.

Maddy lifted a shoulder. "Maybe he's givin' them ideas for the picture."

"He'd better not be."

Maddy laughed. "You're just worried they'll beat your pink bathtubs."

"Nobody'll beat my tubs."

"Uh-huh. Or maybe they're talkin' about what happened between you and Tamel."

Uh-oh.

Jess drew herself up and gave her sister an imperious look. "Nothin' happened between me and Tamel."

"Well, you certainly seem to be gettin' along all of a sudden."

Jess pulled her mouth in and turned away. Which was all that needed to be said. Ruth and Maddy exchanged a glance. Maddy gave a thumbs up. Ruth nodded.

Thank you, Lord.

Ben eventually came downstairs. Ruth fed him a late lunch. Christina didn't so much as poke her head out of her room. Ben ate despondently, then moped around the house. He sought consolation in Ruth and his two sisters, moving from teary-eyed to angry and defensive as he related what had happened. Bottom line, he'd done all he could do. Now it was up to Christina.

The afternoon inched by. Ben kept watching the clock and shooting glances toward the hall. Ruth could not stop thinking about Christina locked in her room. Wasn't she hungry? Shouldn't she take her some lunch?

Ben said no. "She wants to be left alone, and that's what we're gonna do."

"But maybe she's waitin' for us to make the first move."

"I *did* make the first move, Mama. I went to her. And she turned me away." The hurt in Ben's voice pierced Ruth's heart.

The kids, Sy, and Don came inside, cheeks beet red and sweating. "Whoo!" Sy rinsed his face off at the kitchen sink. "I need another shower." The little girls were dragging. Maddy sent them both to their rooms for a nap. Lacey insisted on taking Penny with her. Penny obliged.

Around four o'clock Jake and Sarah returned, apparently victorious in their search. "What did you find?" Maddy started pestering them as soon as they came in the door.

Jake's eyes shone. "Not tellin'."

"Oh, come on!"

"Nope. Just prepare to be amazed."

"Sarah, tell us."

"Huh-uh." She scrunched her nose at Jess and sing-songed, "We're gonna beat you."

"We'll just see about that." Jess wagged her head.

The picture-taking would take place Sunday afternoon. In the morning they'd go to church. Would Christina be with them for any of it? Certainly by tomorrow morning she'd come out of her room. She had to eat.

No matter what Ben said, Ruth wasn't about to let a guest starve.

CHAPTER 24

After Ben stormed out of her room, Christina had cried herself to sleep. When she awoke, her face felt hot and her eyelashes glued together. She pried her lids open and stood up to check herself in the dresser mirror. Drew back her head in horror. She looked absolutely awful. Red eyes and chapped lips. No moisture left in her system.

She desperately needed water. At the bathroom sink she guzzled down two glasses.

After that she couldn't seem to keep still. She paced the room, going 'round and 'round until her legs grew tired and her stomach rumbled. When she sighed herself onto the bench the little gold clock on the dresser read three forty-five.

Christina stared at the carpet, her mind numb. She needed Ben but would never make him happy. Longed for a bright future but didn't know how to let go of her dark past. Wanted to be loved yet was too scared to freely love in return.

Ben's words echoed in her head. *"Are you gonna let your awful past ruin the rest of your life? Or are you willin' to do the work to climb out of it?"* Of course she wanted to climb out of it. But she didn't know *how*. That was just it.

She never should have come. Never have let Ben take her on that first date. She just wanted to die.

Christina knew she should pray. She'd been going to church with Ben and felt peace in God's presence. She'd thanked God many times for sending him to her. Had promised to treat Ben right in return. Now look at her. Why should God listen anyway? Why should he want a thing to do with her?

A little tap came through her bedroom door. Christina didn't answer. Maybe the person would think she was asleep. The knock came again.

She sighed. "Who is it?"

"Lacey."

Christina barely heard the quiet voice.

She pushed herself to her feet and opened the door. Lacey gazed up at her with a solemn face, Penny in her arms. The Yorkie gave Christina the once-over.

Oh, great. The dog that didn't like her.

"Can I come in?" Lacey whispered.

Christina opened the door wider and stepped back.

"Close it quick." Lacey came in and slipped out of sight from the doorway.

Christina shut it. Tilted her head at Lacey. The little girl lifted both shoulders and let them drop. "I'm supposed to be takin' a nap."

196

"Oh."

"But I already took a little one."

"Uh-huh."

"Sort of."

They looked at each other. Christina wanted Lacey to leave but couldn't bring herself to reject her like that. "Want to sit down?"

Lacey nodded and plopped on the bed. Penny settled beside her.

Christina hesitated, then sat down on the other side of the dog, some distance away.

Lacey jiggled on the mattress. "Why are you in here?"

"I was sleeping too."

"Oh. But you're awake now."

"Uh-huh."

"You gonna go out there with Ben?"

"Not yet. I'll stay and talk to you."

Lacey grinned. She pushed her lips together and petted Lady Penelope. Christina merely watched. "Guess what we're havin' for supper," Lacey said.

Christina flinched. That was not a subject she cared to discuss. "What?"

"Hamburgers!" Lacey bounced on the bed.

"You like hamburgers?"

"They're my favorite! Alex's and Pogey's too. We're so glad everyone's gonna eat 'em. So we don't have to see those scary fish things on the plates."

"You mean the lobsters?"

Lacey shuddered. "I think if I saw Daddy eat one, I'd throw up. Or Mama either."

Well. At least Christina had pleased someone in the family.

Lacey watched her own fingers move through Penny's fur. "You can pet her too."

197

"I don't think so. She doesn't like me anymore."

"Yeah she does."

Christina closed her eyes. Lacey sounded just like Ben. Why wouldn't anyone listen to her?

"Why do you think she doesn't like you?"

"I laughed at her when she was howling. She got mad."

"Ohhh." Lacey moved her chin up and down. "And then she went to the corner and pouted?"

"Yes."

Lacey made a face. "She can pout just like Alex."

That was certainly true.

"Anyway, it doesn't mean anything. She gets mad for a while, then she forgets."

"How do you know?"

Lacey scratched Penny behind the ears. The dog closed her eyes and smiled a doggie smile. "She's been mad at all of us at one time. Me too. But look at her now. She's my real friend." Lacey lifted her hand from Penny's head. "Go ahead. You try."

Christina stilled. She didn't want to try. Because if it didn't work, if a stupid *dog* wouldn't even accept her …

"Go ahead, why're you scared? She doesn't bite."

Sometimes words—or doggie actions—bit worse than teeth.

Lacey cocked her head and gazed at Christina. "Are you sad?"

Christina blinked. "Yes," she heard herself say.

"Oh." Lacey started petting Lady Penelope again. "I have a sad friend."

"You do? Who?"

"Kelly."

"Why is she sad?"

"Her mama died."

Christina sucked in a breath. "Oh, that's terrible."

"Mm-hm." Lacey's eyebrows knit. "I try to make her not sad."

"What do you do?"

"Go to her house and talk to her. Give her a colorin' book sometimes. Or new crayons. She really likes it when I do that. And for a little while she's happier, I think. But then she's sad again."

Christina watched her gently ruffle Penny's fur.

"Mama says I can't really make her happy, no matter how hard I try. Only just for a little while."

"Because she's lost someone really important."

"Uh-huh. But I like to see that little while part. I think maybe one day she'll feel better. But Mama says it will take a long time."

Christina couldn't imagine losing someone who really loved her like that.

Wait, what was she thinking? She was losing Ben ...

Lacey looked into Christina's eyes. "Why are *you* sad?"

"I ... just am."

Lacey bit her lip. "Don't you like it here?"

"Sure."

"Do you like me?"

"Are you kidding—I think you're wonderful."

Lacey beamed. She considered Christina a moment longer, than put her little hand on top of Christina's. "Here." She moved Christina's fingers toward Penny. "If you pet her, you'll feel better."

Christina let her hand hover over the Yorkie, barely touching the soft fur. Then she lowered her fingers. Carefully she started petting. At the different touch, Penny opened lazy eyes and looked up at

Christina. Her fingers stilled. Penny's eyes slipped shut again.

"See?" Lacey smiled. "She knows it's you."

Something cracked inside Christina, something small and ... earth shaking.

Lady Penelope rolled on her side and lifted her two top legs.

"She wants you to scritch her belly," Lacey said.

Scritch?

Christina rubbed her fingers across the Yorkie's little stomach. The dog sighed.

Lacey grinned. "See, told you."

"Guess you did."

It was only a dog. And a little girl who couldn't possibly understand. Still, Lacey had such a huge heart. Christina felt her own warming.

Lacey squashed her lips together. "I wish Kelly could forget that easy. So she could feel better."

"Me too." The dog was now completely on her back, all four paws in the air. Christina ran her hand up and down the dog's belly.

Lacey kicked one of her feet. "You know why Penny forgets after somebody's made her mad?"

"Why?"

"'Cause." Lacey raised her hands, palms up. "She'd miss a whole lot of love if she didn't."

The words trickled through the crack inside Christina. Dissolved some of the edges. Her throat tightened. She gazed across the room at the bench where she and Ben had sat. Remembered the swirling pain on his face ...

Her fingers stilled.

She felt a tiny thump on her hand. Penny's eyes had opened, her right front paw tapping Christina's palm—*hey, scritch already.* Christina started petting her again. The dog's eyes closed in sheer bliss.

The crack inside her widened. Something behind it glowed.

"Lacey?" Sarah's irritated voice beyond the door made them both jump. "Are you in there?"

The little girl's eyes rounded. Christina patted her on the arm. "It's okay." She slid off the bed and opened the door.

Sarah looked past Christina at her daughter. "I'm so sorry. Lacey, you are not supposed to be in here botherin' her."

"She's not bothering me. Not at all."

Sarah regarded Christina.

"We were just ... petting Lady Penelope. Lacey was telling me about her friend Kelly."

"Oh." Sarah's expression softened. "Yeah. Sad story." She looked to Lacey. "But come on. You need to come out of there now."

"Is it time for the hamburgers?" Lacey slipped from the bed. Penny stayed behind.

"Not yet."

Sarah glanced at Christina—and caught her eye. They exchanged a long look. Christina felt nothing but concern vibrating from her. No judgment.

"You're comin' out for supper, aren't you?" Sarah asked.

Christina hesitated. "I don't know."

"Yes you are!" Lacey pulled at her arm. "And sit by me."

Sarah offered a small smile. "You know I make a mean after-supper latte."

"No other family will love you like this one—if you'll just quit pushin' 'em away."

201

Christina shifted on her feet. "Won't *anybody* else drink one with you?"

Sarah shook her head. "What do they know anyhow?"

Her expression was so open. Inviting. Caring. Christina didn't know what to do with that.

Sarah reached for Lacey's hand and pulled her out the door. "Listen, Christina. I'm sorry for laughin' about the lobsters. I—*we*—were laughin' at Jess, not you. She was havin' one of her hissy fits."

Tears tugged at the back of Christina's throat. "I … know."

Sarah tapped her daughter on the head. "Go on into our room. Brush your hair."

With a final smile at Christina, Lacey skipped away.

Sarah dropped her voice. "Jess wasn't mad at you either. Not really. I know she acted like it. But it's because she was havin' trouble with Tamel."

Christina raised her eyebrows.

"Looks like they got it worked out now, though. I don't know the details, and Jess isn't about to tell. And don't *you* tell her I said anything."

"Okay." How were they even having this conversation? Christina felt more than a little stunned.

Sarah leaned forward, one conspirator to another. "Tell you somethin' else. But it's a secret."

Christina could only nod.

"Jake and I found the *perfect* spot for our family pictures tomorrow." Her eyes danced. "Jess is gonna die. It's way better than her bathtubs."

"Oh."

"We take the pictures after church. It's always the craziest afternoon of the reunion. Lots of fun." Sarah grinned.

Christina's head bobbed once more. She tried to smile back.

"Well." Sarah straightened. "I'll let you get ready for supper. I think it's in about forty-five minutes." She threw another dazzling smile at Christina. Nothing fake about it. Nothing forced.

"Okay. I'll be there."

Had she said that?

Sarah nodded and walked off. Christina closed her door in a daze.

What had just happened?

She turned around and spotted Penny still lying on the bed. The Yorkie caught her gaze and gave a little wiggle—*come pet me.*

Christina walked to the bed and sat down. Picked up Lady Penelope and held her in her lap. The little dog snuggled in.

Staring at the door, Christina pictured Sarah and Lacey, and the rest of the family. Most of all—Ben.

"Your future belongs with me. Nobody else is gonna love you like I do."

The crack inside Christina opened wider still, and she sensed with a start what the glow behind it was. Hope. She closed her eyes and dwelt in it awhile. Tried to get used to the feel of it. Then she took a deep breath—maybe the deepest of her life. Gently she placed Penny back on the bed and headed into the bathroom to fix her makeup for supper.

CHAPTER 25

Ben sat outside on the porch, the humid heat and his own depression lying heavily on his shoulders. He stared across the road to the field on the other side, remembering times with Christina, wondering if they'd ever happen again. Part of him couldn't believe he'd lose her. Part of him sensed she'd never break out of her hard shell. She didn't know how. And he didn't know how to teach her.

Despite what he'd said to his mother, he'd stopped himself three times from knocking on her door. Demanding a decision.

Ben lowered his head and tried to breathe.

Behind him the house's front door opened. He didn't bother to turn around.

"Ben?" Mama's voice.

"Hmm?" The response came out rough.

"Christina's lookin' for you."

His head jerked up. He swiveled around, searching his mother's face. Did Christina want to work things out? Or would she keep demanding he take her home?

Mom gave him an empathetic but hopeful smile. "She's apologized to Jess."

Ben pushed to his feet, heart tripping. Mama stood back as he hurried into the house.

Christina stood in the kitchen looking worn—and more beautiful than he'd ever seen her. All three of Ben's sisters were nearby, their husbands in the family room, Dad in his chair. Tension and awkwardness swirled through the air, his family trying to act normal, as if Ben's entire future didn't rest on this moment. Christina's body looked tight.

Their eyes locked.

Something—self-consciousness?—flushed her cheeks. "Hi."

"Hi."

No one moved.

"Want to take a walk?" Ben heard himself say.

In the heat? That was crazy.

Christina nodded. She headed toward him—and Ben could have sworn he heard his whole family breathe.

"Sy, time to put the hamburgers on." Mama was back in the kitchen, trying to keep her voice even.

"Okay." Dad rose as if glad for something to do, Jake and Don following. Grilling meat was a man's cooperative sport.

Ben took Christina's hand. They went outside but stopped on the porch, out of the sun. He turned her to face him. "Tell me."

"I ..." Her eyes filled with tears. She shook her head and swallowed. Ben's heart plummeted.

After a time Christina got hold of herself. Wiped her eyes. Her mouth creaked open. "I love you. And I don't ..." Her chin quivered. "I don't want to be alone anymore."

The words ripped through Ben. He slipped his arms around her. Pressed her to his chest.

"I don't know how we're going to do this." Christina spoke into his neck. "But we have to try. *I* have to try."

Ben held her tighter, his eyes squeezed shut. "So do I, just as much as you. But we'll do just fine, you'll see."

For a long time they stood there, neither wanting to move. Finally Ben broke away, leading Christina to sit on the top step where he'd been just minutes— and ages—before. They entwined their arms, at first saying nothing. Just *being*. Ben vacillated between wanting to know what had led to her decision and being afraid to ask. What if she wouldn't tell him? What if she still held back, not trusting?

At some point the question popped out of his mouth. "What happened?"

Christina gazed down the street, biting her lip. Anxiety, then resolve played across her expression. "Kind of hard to explain. It was ... Lacey. And Penny. And Sarah."

Ben pulled his head back. "Really? Sarah talked to you?"

"She came to get Lacey out of my room. Lacey was supposed to be sleeping. And she had Penny."

"Oh." Ben's sister hadn't said a word about that. "So ... what?"

Christina lifted a shoulder. "They said things that got to me. They didn't even know it. And Penny let

207

me pet her again. It was just … I needed …" She shook her head. "It was at the right time, is all."

Ben nodded. "I was prayin'. At least tryin' to."

Christina took a moment to process that. She gave a little smile. "Guess it worked."

He wound his fingers through hers. For a few moments neither of them had anything more to say.

The smell of grilling hamburgers wafted from the backyard. Ben sniffed. "Smells good."

Christina smiled. "Yeah."

"I'm so glad it's hamburgers." Ben made a face. "Don't tell Jess, but I don't even like lobster."

"Really?"

"Really." Ben chuckled. "I'm glad you killed 'em off."

Christina swatted him on the arm.

A car drove by, its window down. The driver, a strange-looking woman with long brown dreadlocks, craned her head at them, then waved. They waved back. "Who is *that*?" Christina asked.

"Rita Betts. Owns the Mocha Ritaville coffee express downtown. Probably just closed up for the day. She lives a couple miles down the road." He shook his head. "Word about us'll be all over Justus tomorrow."

"Really?"

"She'll phone half the town. They'll call the other half."

Christina searched his face. "Is that bad?"

Ben grinned. "Are you kiddin'? My reputation's gonna soar. Prettiest girl this town's ever seen—and she's on my arm. Can't *wait* to show you off at church tomorrow."

Christina leaned into him, her head on his shoulder. A big part of her still cringed at the thought of being on display like that. Everyone in town talking, wanting to get a look at Ben Dearing's fiancée. But a new, small voice whispered *So what? Hold your head high.*

That's the voice she would need to listen to from now on.

CHAPTER 26

Sunday dawned five degrees cooler—a small but welcome relief from the heat. Jess and her family filled a whole church pew, Tamel sitting beside her. She hadn't slept too well the previous night. She and Tamel had gone out for their drive (in his awful car that he'd *have* to get rid of), and ended up closing down a restaurant in Jackson with their second dessert of the evening. They'd talked and talked, Tamel admitting how much he wanted to get out of Justus, resume his life. Yet he felt guilty saying that because of his dad. He was doing the best he could, taking care of a father who hadn't done all that much to take care of him. Jess felt terrible that she'd been so hard on Tamel. She had to admit he was doing a noble thing.

Once the reunion was over, they didn't know when they'd see each other again. Memphis was only four hours away, but Tamel didn't feel like he could leave his dad alone overnight, and Jess was so busy it was hard to get away, even for a weekend.

Somehow, they'd find a way.

In church she barely heard the sermon. She still couldn't quite believe this was happening. Deep inside she'd known it *should*, but her independent spirit hadn't allowed her to do anything about it. Even now, wanting Tamel, she still wanted her independence too. How was that supposed to work?

Meanwhile Ben and Christina sure looked happier. Ben had assured Jess they'd talked things out. Maybe. She still wasn't betting a hundred percent on that relationship.

After church the family had a lunch of cob salad and fruit. The kids ate more hamburgers. Sarah and Jake could barely contain their excitement over leading everyone to The Family Photo site. "You're gonna love it." Jake poked Jess in the shoulder.

"No she won't." Sarah loaded salad on her plate. "She'll be all ticked off about bein' bested."

Tamel was supposed to meet them at the site, serving as picture taker. Which meant he already knew where they'd be.

"Did Tamel give you this idea?" Jess asked Sarah for the fifth time.

"We found it all by ourselves," Jake insisted.

Yeah, right.

After lunch everyone got fixed up to go. Jess chose a soft pink top and white shorts. Glitter sandals. Sarah and Maddy emerged in almost identical blue shirts. "Agh!" Maddy threw her hands up. She disappeared into her room to change.

"What do they care what they're wearing?" Don asked Dad.

"Women and their pictures." Dad shook his head.

Mama came downstairs in multi-colored blue and green. Her eyes sparkled. "This is gonna be fun."

She'd been a lot more lighthearted since Ben and Christina got back together.

Dad grinned at her and did his look-right-look-left thing. Mama scrunched her nose at him and smiled back.

Ben and Christina sat on the couch, Penny perched on Christina's lap. Christina looked great in a turquoise top that matched her eyes. The Yorkie knew something was up, the way people were milling around. Of course, she would be in the picture too.

"All right, everybody here?" Jake stood in the middle of the family room, his fancy camera hanging around his neck. "Time to go."

"Where are we goin'?" Jess and Mama asked at once.

"Just follow us." Jake arched his hand through the air like some Pied Piper.

"We'd better not be climbin' another tree." Maddy put her hands on her hips.

"It's way better than that." Jake looked mighty sure of himself.

They all marched out to the garage. Jess crowded into the backseat of her parents' car along with Christina, Ben, and Lady Penelope. Jake, Sarah, and their two kids took off down the road, leading the procession. Maddy, Don, and Alex were next. Jess's dad backed out of the garage and followed, bringing up the rear. They drove through Justus, past the downtown block, and on up Highway Forty-Nine toward Jackson. Jake had told them the place was about five minutes outside town.

Penny scurried from Christina's lap to Ben's. She put her paws on the door and watched out the window.

Ben had a tight hold on Christina's hand as if he never wanted to let go. He leaned toward the front seat. "Guess what we're talkin' about at supper tonight." He winked at Christina. She gave him a shy smile.

"What's that, Son?" Dad flicked a look in the rear view mirror.

"The wedding date!" Ben waggled his torso, obviously pleased with himself.

"Really?" Mama looked over her shoulder. "That's wonderful! When were you thinkin'?"

"Sooner the better." Ben grinned.

And just why wasn't Christina in on this conversation? Jess turned to look her in the eye. "You're awful quiet about all this."

Ben squeezed his fiancée's hand. "She's just a little—"

"I'm not talking to you."

Christina took a breath. "I'm just … overwhelmed."

Was there a happy in there somewhere?

"Well, don't worry about it now." Ben waved his free hand above Penny's head. "We'll figure it out at supper."

All righty then.

Jess let the subject drop and focused on the cars ahead. After a moment Jake turned left off the highway.

"Oh, no." She made a face. "Tell me we're not goin' to Crazy Eddie's house."

"Crazy Eddie?" Christina mouthed.

"He's a buck-toothed old man with a perpetual garage sale." Just as Jess spotted Crazy Eddie's dumpy-looking property ahead, they started to slow. She closed her eyes. "Oh, man." No telling what she'd get on her pretty sandals, walking around that guy's place.

Jake turned left into the long gravel driveway. Drove up parallel to the rickety red barn and stopped. Crazy Eddie loped out his front door, grinning to beat the band.

"I just know Tamel did this." Jess lasered the cluttered yard with her eyes. "Traitor."

They rolled up the driveway and stopped. With a huge sigh, she got out of the car. Christina slid out behind her. Ben carried Penny.

Up the road came Chiquita Banana. Jess faced Tamel's beastly car, arms folded. He turned into the driveway and slid from the driver's seat, all smiles. "You did this!" Jess pointed at him.

Tamel halted and placed a flat hand against his chest—*Moi?*

Swiveling away from Tamel, Jess scanned Crazy Eddie's yard. The man was already talking a mile a minute, shaking hands with her dad, Jake, and Don. The yard was littered with old couches and chairs, a rusting stove, two worn saddles, an iron bed frame, and who knew what all else. Not one thing worthy of the Dearing Family Photo.

"Thank y'all for comin!" Crazy Eddie stood with his bowed legs wide apart, skinny arms waving like a snake oil salesman. He had a reedy voice from years of smoking. What was left of his gray hair stuck out in all directions, including from his ears. "Hope you'll look around, see somethin' to take home whilst yer here."

Uh-huh. One thing Jess knew about Crazy Eddie. They weren't taking this picture for free.

Tamel sidled up to Jess. She threw him an I-know-you're-in-on-this glance. "How much did Jake pay him for this?" Whatever it was, it was too much.

"How should I know?"

"You know."

"Don't either."

"Do too."

"Do not."

Jess flicked a look at the sky.

The three kids milled around, their mouths open. Alex wore a grossed-out look on her little face. Mama walked up close to Ben, staring at the yard with a nonplussed expression. Lady Penelope scrambled from Ben's arms to hers and clung to her chest. Jess could practically hear her panicked doggie thoughts. *Please don't put me down in all this mess!*

"Okay." Dad looked around. "Where we goin', Jake?"

"Other side of the barn."

Have mercy, there was *more* over there?

They all traipsed around, the kids running ahead. Christina held tightly to Ben's hand. Tamel tried to hold Jess's, but she swatted him away. "Huh-uh, you traitor."

"You know you love me." He stuck his dimpled face in hers, grinning.

One of these days she was gonna throttle him.

The kids rounded the barn first. The girls started screaming. Pogey howled like a hyena.

Mama halted at the edge of the barn and jerked up both arms. "Oh, no." She started laughing.

What in the world? Jess picked up speed, Tamel beside her. She skidded around the dilapidated corner—and saw six old toilets in a row. Two blue, one pink, two white, and one a hideous green. They sat close to one another, the faded wooden slats of Crazy Eddie's barn as a backdrop.

Christina and Ben came up beside Jess, Christina's eyes rounding. "Aw-haw." Ben raised his eyebrows. "That's *great*."

"Ain't they beauties!" Crazy Eddie spread his arms wide.

Don leaned back and guffawed. "Where'd you get 'em?"

"Oh, here and there. They's all fer sale, ever one. Need to fix up a bathroom er two?" Crazy Eddie turned to Mama. "How 'bout you, Little Lady?"

She shook her head. "Not today."

Maddy gazed at the scene as if she suddenly longed to climb a tree. "What are we supposed to do with those things?"

"Sit on 'em, of course." Jake took the camera from around his neck and handed it to Tamel.

Maddy made a face. "Lids stayin' down, I hope."

"Nope, lids up, pants down."

"*What?*"

Crazy Eddie cackled like a wet hen. Everyone else but Maddy dissolved in laughter. Even Jess couldn't help herself. Tamel held his sides. Don pointed at his wife. "Didja see her face?"

"Ha-ha." Maddy threw him a look to kill. "You better be careful, mister. I walk softly and carry a big brick."

Sarah giggled harder. "Stick, Maddy, stick!"

"Oh, *whatever*." Maddy stomped away from the toilets.

Crazy Eddie bent over, then hit the ground, laughing until he wheezed.

217

It took some time for everyone to recover.

"Oh, boy." Jake wiped his forehead. "Okay, let's get settled." He moved front and center of the line-up. "Oldest to youngest." He pointed to the blue toilet at the left end. "Sy, you sit down first, Mama on your lap. She can hold Penny. Sarah and I go second." They'd be on one of the white ones. "Maddy and Don, you next." That would be the ratty green potty. "Jess, you're next, then Ben and Christina." On blue and white. "And the final pink one's for the kids."

Pogey looked more than indignant. "I am *not* sittin' on a toilet with two girls!"

"I'm not sittin' with him, either." Alex put on her best frown.

"How 'bout we pose as families?" Dad said. "Lacey, you can be on your mama's lap. Pogey, you stand beside 'em."

Jake thought that one over. "Who takes the last toilet?"

"Lady Penelope." Mama held up the Yorkie.

"She'll never sit by herself," Ben said.

"Well, we can give it a try." Mama handed Penny to Christina. "Here, you hold her till the last second. Then set her down, see what happens."

Bodies milled about, getting settled. Jess sat down on her closed toilet, feeling conspicuously alone. She leaned toward Christina. "If Penny doesn't stay by herself, I'll hold her."

Tamel stood back, readying the camera. Now and then Crazy Eddie squawked a direction to somebody. "You, there, that's good ... you need to sit forward a little."

Man was probably getting paid by the minute.

"Okay, girls." Jake spoke from behind Sarah's back. "Climb on up on your mama's laps."

The girls scrambled up. Pogey stood at the back of his family's toilet, one hand on his father's shoulder.

"Lookin' good." Tamel eyed them keenly. "Final places. Men, lean left. Women, lean right. Kids, sit straight." He watched as everyone followed his commands.

"Ouch," Maddy protested to Alex. "You kicked me."

"Well, don't hold me so hard." Alex frowned and wiggled.

"Okay, everybody, hold it, hold it." Tamel eyed them all again, Crazy Eddie by his side. "What do you think, Ed?"

"Looks to me like the family's goin' to pot."

Jess threw back her head and hooted. Sarah giggled so hard she dropped Lacey, then fell off her husband's lap. Mama and Dad started in, and soon the whole scene fell apart, people off their toilets. Even Christina laughed. Crazy Eddie trotted around howling like he'd just said the world's biggest joke.

Nobody settled down until they ran out of air. Jess's sides hurt.

"Okay, okay." Tamel was still chuckling. "Let's try this again."

Mama climbed back on Dad's lap. "It's *hard* keepin' this family in line."

"Sure is," Dad said.

"But we manage somehow, don't we?" Mama smiled at him over her shoulder.

"With God's grace, Ruthie. With God's grace."

"Okay, we're almost there." Tamel raised the camera. "Christina, put Penny down."

219

Christina obeyed. Jess leaned around her and Ben to watch. Lady Penelope turned in circles three times on the closed toilet lid. Then, with an air of abundant resignation, she gave the rest of the family a disdainful glance—and sat.

"Perfect," Tamel crowed. "Here, Penny, look here." He shuffled an inch to his right.

Amazingly, the Yorkie faced him.

"Hold it!"

Jess smiled.

Tamel took the shot, and the shutter clicked. Jess imagined the photo, everyone perched on their toilets, looking as regal as a Dearing could.

Tamel checked the photo on the camera. "All right, it looks great. Let's take a few more for good measure." He clicked off a second shot. Moved a few people this way and that an inch or two, then took a third. After a fourth and fifth, he seemed satisfied.

"Can I get up now?" Alex whined.

"Wait a minute." Crazy Eddie reached for the camera. "Let me take one, Tamel. You should be in the picture."

Tamel pointed to himself—*me?*

Crazy Eddie winked at him. "Don't act so innocent. I know where you belong."

With her, no doubt, Jess thought. Which was totally forging new territory, him being in the Dearing Family Photo. She wasn't sure if she liked that or not.

"Yes, come on, Tamel, get in," Mom called.

Fine then, who was Jess to say no? She got up, let Tamel settle, then sat on his lap. His arms circled around her waist. They felt *good*.

"Okay." Crazy Eddie squinted one eye behind the camera. "Men to the left; women to the right, kids straight. Penny, you're perfect."

He took the shot.

Well, that wasn't so bad. Jess turned around and smiled at Tamel. Come Christmas, she just might choose that final picture for the cover of next year's calendar.

If Tamel behaved himself.

CHAPTER 27

At supper—the final meal of the reunion—
Christina sat beside Ben, excitement and more than a
little fear tumbling inside her. Part of her still
couldn't believe this was happening. She was really
going to do this. Marry Ben. Become a member of
the Dearing family for good.

Maybe that last part might be a little too much to
think about right now. One thing at a time.

How glad she was that Ben hadn't taken her
home yesterday. They'd talked a lot since she came
out of her room. She'd told him more about her past.
He'd assured her they'd work through everything.
Starting with the wedding details. But even now the
two selves inside her continued to fight each other.
The old side wanted to please everyone, let them
make the decisions. The other wanted to stand up for
herself, make herself heard. It was her wedding,
wasn't it?

Now, with dessert being served—blackberry cobbler—Ben brought up the subject of the wedding date. "We're thinkin' around Christmas. Here in Justus."

"I wanna be in the wedding!" Lacey tugged at Christina's sleeve. "Can I?"

"Me, too!" Alex bounced in her chair.

Oh, really. Suddenly Alex wasn't so mad about her dirty clothes?

"Well, *I* don't." Pogey happily ate his dessert. "Weddin's are for girls."

"Yeah, and people whose feet don't smell!" Lacey giggled.

Pogey shot his sister a nasty look.

"So you're having it here?" Jess raised her eyebrows. "Not in Dallas? What about all your friends?"

"Can I be in the wedding, *please?*" Alex's eyes shone.

"Alex, be quiet." Don pointed at his daughter.

"But—"

"Quiet."

Christina would love to have Lacey as a flower girl. Alex—not. But she probably couldn't have one without the other.

Ben shrugged. "Our friends who want to attend can come here. We want to be married in our church."

Jess was watching Christina carefully. "You sure you want it here too?"

"Yes. I think it should be in the church where Ben grew up."

There was another reason. It was two states away from her mother.

224

"I'm all for it." Mr. Dearing smiled. "Easier on us."

"December's a good month for me." Sarah dug into her cobbler. "No conferences."

"So what day?" Mrs. Dearing looked to Ben. "Christmas gets so packed."

"How about earlier in the month?" Maddy took a sip of her coffee with obvious pleasure. She'd brewed it, not Sarah. "Like the first weekend?"

"Which would be ..." Jake pulled out his cell phone. "Saturday the sixth?"

"Whoo." Mrs. Dearing sat back in her chair. "Four and a half months away. Can we plan a weddin' that quick?"

"Sure we can." Ben turned to Christina. "What do you think of Saturday the sixth?"

"Sounds good. Between Thanksgiving and Christmas. And yes, we can plan it by then. I don't want a lot of fancy stuff anyway. Simple is fine with me."

"Don't you need to check with your mother?" Maddy asked Christina.

She tensed. She could feel Ben go still. They'd agreed, if this subject came up, she'd answer the way she wanted. He wouldn't do the talking for her. Now she was almost sorry about that.

For a moment she warred with herself. Tell them now? Or leave the subject hanging? Which never seemed to work too well in this family.

She took a deep breath. Two days ago she never in the world could have spoken out like this. "My mother's not invited."

Silence. Christina could feel shock vibrate around the room.

Maddy slowly raised her chin. "Oh."

225

Sarah focused on the table. Don and Jake were suddenly very interested in their cobbler. Ben's parents exchanged sad glances. They'd been told about this already.

Christina's cheeks went hot. She forced herself to look around the table, landing on Jess—the sister hardest for her to get along with. "My mother … is not a nice person. I have as little as possible to do with her. I *don't* want her to ruin my special day. She doesn't care about me anyway."

Jess pressed her lips together, genuine concern in her eyes. "I'm so sorry."

Christina nodded.

The whole family sat for another moment, then seemed to take a collective breath.

"Well." Jake put his cell phone back in his pocket. "Are we set? First Saturday in December?"

Christina and Ben looked at each other, then nodded. He kissed her on the cheek.

"All right then!" Mr. Dearing raised his mug. "A coffee toast!" The adults raised their cups. Pogey, Lacey, and a giggling Alex picked up their water glasses. Mr. Dearing held his higher. "All our love and God's blessings to the happy couple. And welcome to the family, Christina."

"Hear, hear!" Jess, Don, and Jake cheered.

Everyone took a drink.

"Well, that was easy." Mrs. Dearing—Mama Ruth—grinned. "I mean pickin' the date."

Christina smiled. That had certainly been the easiest part of this whole weekend.

"Tell us the truth now, Christina." Maddy clicked her fork against her plate. "After gettin' to know Ben, wasn't meetin' this family the icin' on the pie?"

Jess chortled. "Cake, Maddy."

"Huh?" Maddy frowned. "We're not eatin' cake."

"We're eatin' cobbler," Pogey said.

"And there's no icin' on it, either." Don elbowed his wife.

"Oh, for heaven's sake." Maddy huffed. "You know what I mean."

Christina and Ben leaned into each other and laughed. The laughter felt good. Cleansing.

Maybe Maddy was right—meeting the Dearings was like "the icing on the pie." Unexpected. Different. A little more than she'd bargained for.

But in the end ... something she could get used to.

Mr. & Mrs. Syton Dearing

**request the pleasure of your company
at the marriage of their son**

Benjamin Scott Dearing
to
Christina Renee Day

**Saturday, the sixth of December
two thousand and thirteen
two o'clock in the afternoon**

**New Life Church
118 Wilmington Street
Justus, Mississippi**

Reception to follow

Watch for the second Dearing
Family book, *Pitchin' a Fit.*
The wedding is planned to be
picture perfect, and the family has
once again gathered.
What could possibly go wrong?

A NOTE FROM BRANDILYN

Readers ask me, "Is the Dearing Family series based on your real childhood family?" Others wonder, "Why is the author known for her Seatbelt Suspense® now writing Southern family fiction?"

Okay, okay, if you really wanna know ...

Is the Dearing Family series based on your family?

No and yes. Mostly no. Here's a list of factoids:

I grew up in a small town in Kentucky, population about 3000. Its "downtown" consisted of one block, much like the downtown in my fictional Justus, Mississippi.

My family does love getting together for reunions. And we're a close family. However, we don't argue like the Dearings do. In fact, we get along so well, we'd make a rather boring book. And we're not as loud as the Dearings, either. (My niece Laura says that last sentence is a lie.)

My mother's name is Ruth. To many outside the family she's known as Mama Ruth. Ruth Dearing is like my mom in a couple of ways: my mother tends to be a worrier, and she's warm and loving—a true friend to all.

I have three sisters—six, eleven, and fifteen years older than I. (Clearly, my parents saved the best for last.) None of the Dearing family members are named after my sisters or are based on them.

There are no boys in our family. Hence, Ben is also fictional.

Christina is an entirely fictional character as well.

My sisters and I used to play Liverpool Rummy when I was a kid. Later we got into Scrabble, which we've now played for years. We're competitive. And good. *Don't* play Scrabble with us. You'll die.

Lady Penelope was my childhood dog. However, she was a Chihuahua, not a Yorkie. The personality quirks she possesses in this book are straight out of Penny's real doggie life. Except for sighing about having to go to her bed while the family eats. That quirk was taken from another dog of mine named Mallie.

Much of the food the Dearings eat is from my childhood. My mother is a wonderful cook. At the time of this writing (December 2012), Mom just celebrated her 96th birthday. She lives in an assisted living apartment and no longer has to cook for herself. But she misses it.

My mother made pickled watermelon rind. I liked it as a kid. Although I suppose it's an acquired taste.

Mom also made incredible buttermilk biscuits. And fried chicken and gravy. And sausage with biscuits. And apple pie. Family reunions have been a time of lip-smacking weight gain.

Yes, there is a coffee snob in our family—me. I take my own coffee to reunions and years ago bought an espresso maker to leave at my parents' house. My coffee is always too strong for everyone else. When I make it, they'll pour it into a cup, then water it down. There's just no accounting for taste.

No one in my childhood family played golf. My dad coached soccer and played tennis. He managed to play doubles tennis until he was 84. He passed away from Parkinson's at the age of 88.

My father did not own a car dealership, far from it. He was a missionary, then a professor of missions at a seminary.

My family does have strong Christian roots and beliefs, as do the Dearings.

My husband, Mark, and I follow the same marriage principles of Sy and Ruth: place God in the center and put each other's needs before our own. As Ben said: this takes two.

Remember Syton Dearing's look-right-look-left silent message to Ruth that she's the prettiest in the room? That comes straight from my husband. Like Syton, when we first started dating, Mark would look around and say, "You're the prettiest one here." Years ago the words were no longer needed. He can send me the message across a room—and still does.

For years I've been gathering family photos and putting them into a calendar, which I give each family member for Christmas. Each summer reunion I try to come up with a new crazy venue for taking a picture of my mother and us four daughters. One year it was pink bathtubs at the Habitat for Humanity Restore. Another year is was—yup, you guessed it. Lined-up toilets. I've had a hard time topping that one ever since.

There is no one in my family with horrendously smelly feet like Pogey. For this I am grateful.

Years ago a friend told me of someone he knew in a Southern town who drove a banana yellow hearse. I filed that away in my brain, knowing someday I'd use it in a book.

I used to know a couple named Christina and Ben.

Like Lacey, my little great-niece Breanna takes dancing lessons and tends to walk around on her toes.

Breanna's mother—my niece—is named Jessica. Jess for short.

I have always loved mixed metaphors and other mangled sayings, and was waiting for the day I could create a character who tended to say them without realizing it.

A good friend did once say to me, "That's like putting the cart before the egg." I still think that's the greatest mixed metaphor ever.

Syton Dearing looks like my next-door neighbor.

In the town where I now live is a coffee express named Mocha Ritaville. I don't know the owner. But I've convinced myself she's a woman named Rita in her mid-fifties or so who loves Jimmy Buffett.

The lobster story really did happen—in the household of my oldest sister.

I heard the dead rabbit story from a friend and later learned that snopes.com says it's an urban legend. Whether or not it really happened to Tamel Curd is up to you to decide.

There are no lawyers in our family. There is a doctor (my oldest sister). I was supposed to be the attorney. Every family should have a doctor and a lawyer, don't you think? Makes life so much more convenient. But somewhere I took a wrong turn and ended up writing fiction. Maybe that's not so far off from being a lawyer after all ...

Why are you writing Southern family fiction in addition to your trademarked Seatbelt Suspense®?

When I first began to be published in fiction in 2001, I was writing in both the suspense and women's fiction genres. After a three-book women's fiction series—the Bradleyville series—I turned to writing suspense full time. But I always had a hankering to return to women's fiction. I love exploring relationships, especially those of family in small towns. In fact I had the idea for the Dearing Family series way back when I wrote in both genres, and the books were contracted with my publisher. When the publisher's marketing team and I decided I should write only suspense, the Dearing Family books were set aside. Now that today's technology makes self-publishing so easy, I'm able to write both my contracted Seatbelt Suspense® and my Dearing Family series. And yes (in case you're wondering), I have my publisher's blessing to do so.

As for my Seatbelt Suspense®, those books are written with a four-point brand promise in mind: fast-paced, character-driven suspense with myriad twists and an interwoven thread of faith. You can read more about them, including the first chapter of each, on my website. (See below.)

I've got a crazy story you should use in one of your books!

You do? Great! E-mail the story to me, giving me permission to use it, and you just might see it show up in a novel.

Ways to contact me:

Website: www.brandilyncollins.com. You can e-mail me from that site, plus sign up for my Sneak Pique newsletter, sent via e-mail every other month. You can also read the first chapters of all my published books—and check out what's coming next.

On Facebook I keep in daily contact with readers: www.facebook.com/brandilyncollinsseatbeltsuspense

On Twitter I'm @Brandilyn.

Turn the page to read the first chapter of my suspense novel *Double Blind*.

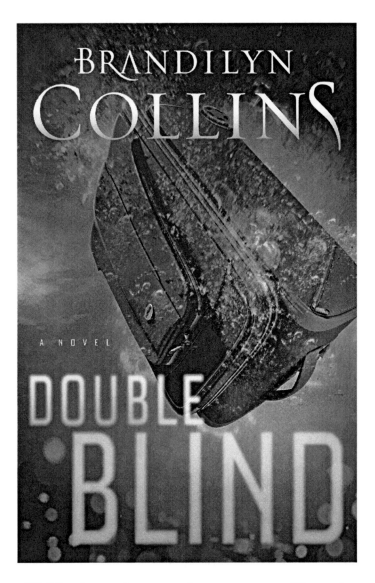

BRANDILYN
COLLINS

A NOVEL

DOUBLE
BLIND

"Collins has written another taut, compelling tale
of psychological suspense that weaves
a twisty plot with threads of faith."
--Library Journal, Starred Review

DOUBLE BLIND

CHAPTER 1

Desperate people make desperate choices.

In my kitchen I took one look at the envelope in the stack of mail and dropped it like burning metal. It landed askew on the counter, the gold Cognoscenti logo pulsing up at me.

If I had known, I would have trashed it right then and there.

Nine months before The Letter arrived, my husband had been killed in a car accident. Ryan, with his lanky body and loving touch, that dimple in his right cheek. His quirky smile and teasing way. He'd been only thirty-five — six years older than I. Four months after his funeral a robber attacked me in a mall parking lot and nearly choked me to death before a security guard happened by. My attacker

i

got away. He's still out there somewhere, walking the streets. And during the two years before Ryan's death? I'd had three miscarriages.

Five traumatic events in a row. I was bent, near broken. A wind-battered sapling. Abandoned by God.

Have you ever battled depression? That black, biting maw that devours you whole and turns your world to darkness? Your life becomes unlivable. You become ... nothing. One day you're a speck in the universe, blown here and there. Trod underfoot. The next you're weighted and shackled, the chains too heavy to lift.

The envelope looked thin, maybe one sheet of paper inside. A single piece of paper that could alter the very core of me.

One last hope.

My fumbling hands picked up the envelope. I slid a finger under the flap and edged it open. Pulled out the answer on which I'd hung my future.

Dear Lisa Newberry,

It is my pleasure to inform you that you have been accepted into the medical trial for Cognoscenti's new Empowerment Chip. Please call our research director at your earliest convenience to set up an appointment so we may proceed. The number is below.

Dr. William Hilderbrand,
President and CEO

Oh. *Oh.*

Weakness rushed me. I leaned against the tile, relief exploding in my chest. Heat blew through my limbs. This was *it*. I was in. I could be whole. My mind could hardly contain the thought.

Not until that moment had I realized the true depth of my despair. If this had been a *No*, who knows what I would have done.

My next thought was of Ryan. *I know you would want this for me.*

And then—it all blitzed away. The euphoria melted as quickly as it had come. In its place, the inevitable pessimism of depression. No way could I be so fortunate. Surely I'd read the letter wrong.

I read it again. A third time, daring the answer to change, knowing it would. But no. The word *accepted* burned from the page.

Excitement rose again, propelling my hand to the phone, sitting next to me on the counter. I picked it up and called Sherry Grubacker, my one friend in the Bay Area. The news trembled on my tongue, ready to jump as soon as she said hello.

Her canned voice mail kicked on. No Sherry.

Well, of course. With such incredible news as this, how could I expect to find someone to share it with?

I hung up.

Next thing I knew I was punching in my mother's number—a reckless choice in the passion of the moment. My mother had known nothing of my many screening interviews with Cognoscenti, the physical and mental work-ups. She'd only nagged me for my weakness in the past few months. Wasn't it time I pulled myself together? She'd had her own difficulties in her lifetime, she reminded me. Losing her husband when I was only two. But she'd managed to throw back her shoulders and move on. Raise me alone.

True. And she'd criticized me the entire time.

What was I *doing*? My finger slowed, then hovered over the last digit. My mother would never condone this decision.

I dropped the receiver back in its cradle. Then slumped over the counter, hands to my temples, feeling adrift. The familiar ennui settled in, dragging along its chilling companion—fear.

Reality clunked in my chest, and I tried to breathe around its weight. The gleaming promise of the letter dulled before my eyes. Cognoscenti's prize had seemed so miraculous while I pursued it. But now that it was within my reach—what was I doing?

No way could I go through with this.

I wandered into the living room of my corner apartment. Gazed through the front window at the sun-strewn afternoon. Early March in Redwood City, California, and the daffodils were up, the magnolia trees in pink bloom. Spring was coming. Renewal time.

For nature, maybe. Not for me.

I pressed cold hands against my cheeks. Brain surgery. *Brain surgery, Lisa.* How could I even think of putting myself through that?

But the procedure was simple, they said. Cognoscenti's advancements in brain chip implants went far beyond any other company's research. If I got the real implant I would instantly escape my whirlpool of defeat. A short stay in the hospital, and I could be a new person. Imagine... nurturing all the memories of Ryan without the deadening grief. Imagine recalling my attack with head knowledge only, not the sucking, terror-drenched memory from my gut.

Who wouldn't want to turn off their pain?

iv

But it wasn't quite that simple.

In what they called the "gold standard" of research — double-blind, placebo-controlled — I could end up with the placebo. The blank chip. The surgery done — for nothing. Amazing they would put people through such turmoil. But that's the way medical research worked.

Still, it was a chance. One little Empowerment Chip, and I could have the strength to rebuild my life. I could *feel* again. Breathe again. If I didn't try it, what future did I have?

I dropped my head in my hands. I wanted this. How very much I needed the hope. Without it I didn't know how to go on.

But what if something went wrong?